Masters

Whenever I think that Sierra Cartwright has out done herself with a previous book, she proves me wrong time and time again... Seriously, if you want to dive into the BDSM genre then you need to start with Sierra Cartwright's Mastered series.
~ *Blackraven's Reviews*

This very spicy read gives a beautiful exposition of one woman's journey into an erotic world that she knew very little of... There are very hot scenes that demonstrate some of the techniques that can be applied but this is also a delicious love story and I look forward to reading more titles from this gifted author. ~ *Night Owl Romance*

The pace was brisk enough, and the sex was spicy and molten... Over the Line is a delicious erotic read for all fans of BDSM. ~ *Fallen Angel Reviews*

Totally Bound Publishing books by Sierra Cartwright:

Mastered
With This Collar
On His Terms
Over the Line
In His Cuffs
For the Sub

Signed, Sealed & Delivered
Bound and Determined
Her Two Doms

Anthologies
Naughty Nibbles: This Time
Naughty Nibbles: Fed Up
Bound Brits: S&M 101
Subspace: Three-way Tie
Night of the Senses:Voyeur
Bound to the Billionaire: Bared to Him

Seasonal Collections
Halloween Hearthrobs: Walk on the Wild Side
Homecoming: Unbound Surrender

Clasndestine Classics
Jane Eyre

Mastered

IN THE DEN

SIERRA CARTWRIGHT

In the Den
ISBN # 978-1-78184-687-2
©Copyright Sierra Cartwright 2013
Cover Art by Posh Gosh ©Copyright 2013
Interior text design by Claire Siemaszkiewicz
Totally Bound Publishing

Published in 2013 by Totally Bound Publishing, Newland House, The Point, Weaver Road, Lincoln, LN6 3QN, United Kingdom.

IN THE DEN

Dedication

For Jason and Catrina, with thanks for the insights.
Scarlett, you are a source of constant inspiration.

Chapter One

Damien Lowell always got what he wanted. Granted, sometimes the challenge was greater than he anticipated. But that didn't matter. The more difficult the task, the more he relished it. Working hard for something flexed his mental muscles, sharpened his senses and fed his creative energy.

Right now he was standing with his arms folded across his chest, his focus on the gorgeous dark-haired Domme on the other side of the room.

Tonight she'd used kohl liner and false eyelashes to add drama and depth to her startling green eyes. Her hair hung over her shoulders and cascaded down her back in a shining mahogany waterfall. She wore thigh-high black boots with heels so tall he was amazed she could walk in them. Fishnet stockings were attached to a garter belt, and her tiny black skirt barely covered her buttocks. She'd topped the breath-taking outfit with a leather corset that he itched to unlace.

As if sensing his perusal, she glanced over and raised her glass in salute. He inclined his head in acknowledgment.

As she sipped, she continued to regard him.

This was a bit of an unusual circumstance for him at the Den. He'd bought the massive mountain estate years before, and he'd turned it into a private and exclusive BDSM club. While female dominants were welcomed and accorded the respect due their position, less than two dozen had applied for membership.

Most of the women he associated with here were subs. They didn't meet and hold his gaze like Mistress Catrina was doing.

After several seconds, she severed the contact and returned her attention to her submissive. She snagged a canapé and offered it to the bare-chested man kneeling before her. Since he sported spikey blond hair, the pair presented a striking contrast.

The man, on a leash and wearing nothing other than tight, gold-colored shorts, looked up at her adoringly. She smiled and brushed a hand across his forehead. She drew him in closer, then popped the treat into his mouth.

All the while, Damien pictured the Domme on her knees, affixed to *his* leash, fully understanding what it meant to submit.

He'd known her for several years and he knew she was an excellent Mistress. Recently she'd attended a private event he'd hosted. That evening, he'd witnessed a deeper, more contemplative side of her. At one point, she'd stood in front of a window, gazing into the distance. When he'd joined her, she'd faced him. For a moment, before she'd schooled it away, he'd seen a groove between her sculpted eyebrows. When he'd asked how she was enjoying the evening, she'd responded with politeness. But she'd excused herself and left soon after.

Damien didn't often allow his thoughts to be consumed by women, especially dominant ones. But since that night, he hadn't been able to get thoughts of Mistress Catrina out of his mind.

"How's it going, Boss?"

Damien turned his attention to the Den's second-in-command, Gregorio. Hiring the man had been one of the smartest business decisions Damien had ever made. Gregorio lived onsite in a caretaker cottage. He ensured the safety of their guests, and he oversaw the estate when it was open for a production company's use. Additionally, he managed the calendar, the employees, the accounting and maintenance. Since he could top or bottom, he was even more valuable to the house.

Gregorio folded his arms across his chest. Tonight he had on a black T-shirt beneath a leather vest. With his silver earring and motorcycle boots, he looked suitably intimidating. "Your demonstration starts in fifteen minutes, Boss." He hooked a thumb and pointed over his shoulder. "Good turnout."

They'd had plenty of reservations for the annual open house extravaganza. "There are a lot of new faces," Damien agreed.

"And buttocks," Gregorio added with a grin.

Despite a widespread snowstorm, guests had arrived from all over the region, including parts of Wyoming, Kansas, even Montana. Gregorio had planned ahead, reserving a block of hotel rooms in the nearby ski town of Winter Park. Skilled staff shuttled people back and forth in four-wheel-drive vehicles.

"Susan went to the ladies' locker room to prepare. She'll meet you in the entranceway. Your items are laid out on the mantel as requested."

Damien nodded. "Great job, as always."

"All in a day's work," Gregorio said. "I'll be assisting you onstage." With a nod, he excused himself.

Mistress Catrina was no longer in sight, and Damien wondered if she'd taken her submissive downstairs to one of the private rooms.

Demonstrations typically drew a number of neophytes and people curious about joining the club. During presentations, long-time members often took advantage of the uncrowded conditions in the dungeon to connect and scene.

He went upstairs to his private suite and flicked on the fireplace to banish the winter chill. The blinds were open and snow drifted past the massive windows. Another stunning Colorado night, cold and windy, perfect for sleep—or other things—in his custom-built bed.

In the backyard area, the fire pit blazed and a few well-dressed, hearty souls stood around it.

After changing into black leather pants and a short-sleeved T-shirt, he clipped a whip to his side and went back down the stairs in time to see Mistress Catrina while she was still in the public area. He tried not to show how ridiculously pleased he was. "Milady," he said by way of greeting.

"Damien," she returned, glancing at him through long, enhanced lashes.

He wondered what she looked like natural, naked, on her knees, her lips trembling as she waited for him. Then he shoved the thought away. No sense allowing his imagination free rein. He'd enjoyed success in business because he was pragmatic, not fanciful. "Enjoying the evening?" he asked.

"Of course."

"I'll take that as a polite lie."

She scowled. "Your events are always fabulous."

"So why aren't you having a good time?"

"You're the one who said I'm not," she countered.

Her scent was as exotic as she was. Musk and vanilla, layered with a pervasive sexual need. He wondered if he was the only one who noticed it. "Where's your boy?"

"He's outside having a smoke. Bad habit," she said. "But who am I to judge?"

"Who, indeed?"

"We only hooked up for part of the evening."

"That collar isn't yours?"

"No. I've never formally collared anyone. That particular one belongs to Master Lawrence. We're hoping he makes it up here tonight." She shrugged, her creamy shoulders rising and falling before settling into a gentle slope.

"But with the weather…"

A sudden urge to wrap his fingers around her upper arms and drag her to her toes assailed Damien. But that would violate personal as well as house rules. He owed her the same respect accorded to all dominants. In all his years of being a Dom, he'd never had the urge to drive a Domme to her knees. Until now. "Are you planning to attend my demo?"

"No," she said.

When he'd first met her, he'd decided she was blunt. Over time, he'd learned to appreciate her honesty. "Perhaps you should."

She tilted her head. "You think you can teach me something?"

"A lot of things," he said.

"That's a bit arrogant, Damien."

He longed to hear the word Sir on her lips. "Is it? We can all benefit from continuing education."

"Setting the scene and an intro to flogging is for newbies."

"Really?"

"Have you heard complaints from my subs?" The words were tight, as if her breath were constricted.

"Not at all."

"Then?"

"I'm simply suggesting that some of the best dominants have embraced or at least tried submission."

"As you have?"

"Indeed."

Her mouth parted before she pursed her lips.

"I'd be happy to master you, Catrina."

"If you ever crave a beating, Damien, I'd happy to put the smack down on you," she returned.

"I invite you to try, Milady."

Bradley entered through the kitchen door, and when Catrina saw him, she smiled. Damien wondered what it would be like to see that same expression directed at him.

The man shook snow off his gold boots before joining them. He knelt then placed his forehead on the floor in front of Catrina. "Good boy," she told him, crouching to rub his head.

Damien took Catrina's arm to help her up. Her skin was warm, inviting. If she felt the same jolt of electricity as he had, she hid it well. Against her ear, so no one else could hear, he said, "With your hair, you'd look stunning in that position."

She drew her dramatic eyebrows together as she scowled at him. Without a word, she extracted herself from his grip.

Just then, Master Lawrence arrived and joined them, nodding at Damien and kissing Catrina on the cheek.

"You're here, Master!" Bradley exclaimed.

At Lawrence's urging, the boy thanked Catrina as she relinquished the leash. The blond followed his master down the stairs at an enthusiastic trot.

"I'm available if you change your mind," Damien said to Catrina before moving off to meet his partner in the foyer.

Catrina might have muttered something about Hell freezing over, and with the snow and cold, he figured anything was possible. He grinned. Victory would be a sweet reward.

* * * *

When Damien disappeared from sight, Catrina exhaled. Damn him. Who the hell did he think he was? His words had shaken her, and she glanced around to be certain no one had overheard his outrageous proposition. As if she'd be on her knees for any man.

So what was it about him that sent flutter-kicks through her stomach?

Catrina had always prided herself on being in charge. From class president in high school to editor of the college paper, and now, as the founder of her own company where she focused on the financial success of women, she'd always been outspoken and driven.

After the end of her engagement five years before, she'd gathered up the shattered pieces of her heart and resolved to be in charge of her own life. She'd also made the choice to be equal in her sexual partnerships. Her first experience in taking the initiative with a new man hadn't been well received. Even now she cringed at the memory.

It had taken her a couple of years to move on after her engagement. She'd finally started dating a nice, agreeable man. In the bedroom, though, he'd bored her. No way could she live with the same unimaginative, missionary-style every night. So she'd boldly tied Todd's wrists to a slat in the headboard, and when she'd straddled his face, he'd demanded to be released. Feeling awkward but not deterred, she'd let him go.

For the first time in their relationship, she'd seen an angry side of Todd. He'd towered over her and yelled—she didn't want to be an equal, she was a control freak.

His words had shocked her. He was probably right, but she wouldn't admit it, so she'd met his gaze and disagreed. In response, he'd captured her hands and offered to tie her up and force her to lick his balls. She'd told him to get the hell out.

The next day, when she'd arrived home from work, his few belongings had been gone from her apartment and his key had been sitting in the middle of the dining room table.

A couple of weeks later, she'd met a handsome blond man at a party. After hearing about her previous, disastrous relationship, he'd said he'd kiss her feet. It had turned out he wasn't joking.

Ever since, she'd been involved with good-looking men who took care of her every sexual need. She ensured they received everything they wanted and needed, too. What could be better?

At times, especially in the middle of the night, she pushed away the nagging voice that whispered she was missing intimacy. She'd toss and turn, telling herself she had friends for problem solving and conversation. Her life was full in every way. She didn't need anyone to hold her and connect with about everyday life events. And she didn't need someone like Master Damien Lowell bossing her around and making her kiss his feet. Definitely not.

Gregorio moved through the rooms, announcing the start of Master Damien's demonstration. Now that Master Lawrence had claimed Bradley, Catrina was at loose ends. She could avail herself of the services of a house sub, and maybe even Gregorio with his pirate-like looks, silver earring and sexy body would agree to play with her. Since he was busy talking to a couple she'd never seen before, that would have to wait until later.

More out of boredom than curiosity, and not because Damien had issued a challenge, she snagged a sparkling water infused with cranberry juice and wandered into the living room.

The room's usual furniture had been removed. A couple of rows of fold-up chairs had been arranged in a semicircle near the fireplace. Many dominants were seated, and their subs were standing or kneeling near them.

Catrina stood near the back. From here, she had a clear view of Damien and the pretty sub on her knees, facing him, her head bowed. Catrina appreciated the woman's lush, feminine form. She wore her hair in a blonde bob that shaded her face. The pair were turned sideways to the room, so that both of their expressions and all Damien's gestures were obvious.

Gregorio entered and stood near Damien.

The gathered crowd quietened as Damien touched the woman's head.

Even from the distance, Catrina saw the submissive tremble. It took courage to participate in a demo, especially with the house owner. Her nervousness radiated in the room.

Catrina noticed his biceps flex as he made tiny, massaging motions. His silent communication was impressive.

"I'd like you to stand," he told the woman. "And tell us your name."

"Susan, Sir." She kept her eyes on the wooden floorboards, even as he offered a hand to help her up.

Warmth shimmied up Catrina's spine as she remembered the feel of his firm grip on her arm. She didn't normally accept help, and it had surprised her how much she'd liked it.

"I appreciate your show of respect," he said.

Damien had not used that tone with her. He'd spoken to her as an equal, not as a man intent on seducing a woman.

"And I'd like you to look at me," he continued.

The woman glanced up, her eyes wide and unblinking.

"I want you to be completely comfortable with everything we do here tonight."

"Yes, Sir."

In that same, reassuring voice he went on, "Is there anything you're uncomfortable with?"

"I'd like to leave on my panties, Sir," Susan whispered with her head turned.

He took her chin and recaptured her gaze. "Of course you may leave on your panties. Anything else I can do to reassure you?"

She shook her head but started to fold her arms.

"It appears there may be something else you're reluctant to tell me."

"Ah… I have very sensitive nipples, Sir."

"Then I'll treat your nipples with all due respect."

"Thank you, Sir." She gave a tentative smile.

"And do you have a safe word, Susan?"

"Stop."

"So, to be clear, stop means *stop*."

"Yes, Sir."

"And a slow word?"

"Slow, Sir."

"Got it. We'll take a break if you use the word slow."

"Thank you, Sir."

"You're also aware that 'halt' is the house safe word?"

"Yes, Sir."

In that instant, Catrina understood why Damien taught demos at the open house events. It was one thing to inform Doms that they needed to make their sub feel comfortable, but Damien was a genius. He was repeating what Susan said, but not in parrot-fashion. He soothed and built trust not only with the way he spoke but with physical touch. It was subtle and elegant. Maybe he had been correct in thinking she could learn something from him, as much as that thought rankled.

Transfixed, she took a drink while she watched him undress Susan. He could have ordered the sub to strip. Instead, he squeezed her shoulders and ran his fingers over the skin he bared. "Now I'd like to remove your bra."

Catrina gulped. The seduction in his tone made her wish the words were directed at her.

"Yes, Sir," Susan said.

He turned Susan so that her back was to him.

After he'd released the clasp, he turned her once again. Her shoulders were rolled backwards so that the bra remained in place.

"Thank you for your trust," he continued, drawing the straps down her arms. "Remember you can stop or slow down at any time." When he'd removed the lacy black brassiere and handed it to Gregorio, Damien put his hands on her and said, "You're beautiful, Susan."

As if a switch had been turned on, she smiled, and her cheeks flushed with color, making her look radiant. Hesitancy had been replaced with confidence, impressing Catrina.

She couldn't look away even if she wanted to, as he cupped Susan's breasts and flicked his thumbs across her nipples. Her eyes closed. As he continued, she moaned and moved toward him, curling her fingers around his wrists.

Catrina clutched her glass.

Shock tightened her throat. Damien's concentration seemed riveted on Susan. It appeared as if neither of them were aware of the dozens of people observing them.

For the first time, Catrina saw submission and dominance from an entirely different perspective. For them, nothing seemed to exist outside of one another, and Damien's attention didn't wander from the woman under his care.

Catrina took care of her men, meeting their needs. In return, she had at least one magnificent climax. Until now, that had been enough.

"Tell me what you want, Susan."

"An orgasm, Sir."

He smiled. "Oh, you'll most certainly earn that."

"Thank you, Sir." Her knees buckled.

"Can you wait?" he asked.

"If it's your desire, Sir."

"You're a very pleasing submissive. Tell me what we're demonstrating this evening."

"A flogging, Sir."

"I'd like to make love to you with my flogger," Damien said.

As if she were the one standing in front of him, Catrina's insides melted. The man had hypnotic appeal.

"Yes, Sir."

Catrina had never looked at a man the way Susan was looking at Damien, eyes wide with trust and reverence.

Damien led Susan to the hearth and placed her hands on the mantel. "Legs farther apart for me," he said, his words like a caress.

Susan moved into position.

"I can secure you in place, if you'd like?"

"I'll remain as I am, Sir, if that's okay with you?"

"Perfect," he replied.

She looked lovely, wearing only her panties. She'd been trembling earlier, but now she was still. Though Catrina would never admit it, Damien's power held her spellbound.

Damien had said he wanted to make love to her with his flogger, and that's exactly what he seemed to do. He started with tender leather kisses, licking at the woman's shoulders and back. He let the strands fall in gentle waves.

Catrina had never wielded a handle with such skill. She told herself it was because a man's skin was much tougher than a woman's, but now she questioned whether she'd assumed too much.

She watched as he brought Susan's body to life. He increased the intensity of his blows on her panty-covered buttocks. Her cries were whimpers of desire, not of distress. She appeared to surrender not only to Damien but to the flogger.

Goosebumps rose on Catrina's arms, and her skin tingled with anticipation. And she knew one thing. She didn't want to watch Damien please another woman.

Confused by the irrational thoughts careening through her, she gulped the last of her drink then slammed the empty glass down and headed toward the foyer.

"I'd like to be on the next shuttle to Winter Park," she told the submissive.

"It will be about twenty minutes, Milady. Jeff's just on his way back now."

Catrina nodded, said thanks then found the women's locker room. The place was empty, and she exhaled in relief. She took several minutes to smooth her hair, straighten her skirt, adjust her corset and splash cool water onto her face.

All that done, she felt more in control. She pulled back her shoulders and stepped into the hallway. Damien stood there, overwhelming the space, blocking her way.

She started to take an instinctive step back, but managed to stop herself.

Power cloaked him. Before sanity returned, she wondered what it would be like to play with him.

"You were there," he said. "At the demonstration."

"I had nothing better to do."

"What did you think?"

She shrugged. "You know what you're doing."

"Weren't you curious to know what it would be like to be in her position?"

"Not at all. I can have a gorgeous man at my feet and tell him exactly what to do."

"Is that what you want? Or do you want a man who will concentrate all his efforts on pleasing you?"

"I have that now."

"Do you?" he countered. "Do your men give you the attention I gave Susan?"

"Of course."

"You ought to be taken to task for your lack of honesty."

She shivered. With a stubborn tilt of her chin she snapped back, "How dare you?"

"You looked down and to the left before answering," he said. Then, softer, seducing her with his voice, despite the nature of their conversation, he continued, "When was the last time anyone cared enough to watch your movements so intently that they knew you were lying? Do all your relationships exist strictly on the surface? Do you give no one a piece of your soul?"

His questions wormed their way inside her. They were the same ones that she ran away from. When they caught up to her, she turned up the volume on her television or distracted herself on her elliptical machine, music blaring from ear buds.

"Aren't you curious about what you're missing?"

"No."

"Another lie?"

She shook her head quickly. Too quickly.

He dropped his arms and advanced toward her. This time, she retreated. "Damien..."

"You know the house safe word," he told her. "You can use it at any time. But you aren't going to, are you?"

Jesus. *God.* What the hell was happening here?

Her back was to the wall. This close, she was overwhelmed by his masculine scent and determination.

His blue eyes were as dark as a twilight sky. A tiny pulse in his jaw mesmerized her.

"Is your pussy wet, Milady?"

"From what? Being near you? Watching your little demo? Not at all." His words suffocated her. And her pussy *was* wet. Damn it.

Impossibly, he took another step closer. With one hand, he captured her wrists and pinned them above her.

Her chest rose and fell as emotions tumbled through her. She shouldn't want to interact with him. With Susan, he'd been gentle, but there was nothing soothing in the way he held her, overwhelmed her. But, just as he had watched the other woman, he was directing that same intensity at her, figuring out what she wanted, how she preferred to be dealt with.

He touched the knuckles of his free hand to her throat.

She kept her eyes wide, pretending she wasn't affected.

His touch was so gentle that she hardly felt it. Continuing, Damien skimmed down the center of her chest, bare skin to bare skin.

Then he traced beneath her right breast. He held her gaze, not blinking. She'd never had anyone's attention like this, and it was heady.

Even through her outfit, her nipple hardened when he moved over it.

There wasn't a part of her that wasn't aware of him.

"Open your mouth."

"Why?"

"Because I'm going to kiss you."

She started to protest, but he dove inside her. She expected him to coax her. Instead, he consumed her.

He forced his way in, tasting of an intoxicating blend of persuasion and dominance. The thrusts of his tongue made her mouth water. He insinuated a thigh between her legs, and despite her resolve, she rubbed herself against him.

The woman in her recognized his mental as well as physical strength. This was a man powerful enough for her to trust. He'd never push her too far, but he would demand everything, that she hold nothing back, and maybe give more than she ever had to anyone.

As impossible as it was to believe, he deepened the kiss. She couldn't breathe. Couldn't think. And suddenly she didn't want to.

She felt an orgasm start to unfurl.

A Dom and sub moved past them, and Damien never allowed his attention to wander.

He kissed her until she began to shake.

As quickly as he'd started, he eased away. He adjusted their positions and hiked up her skirt. He moved a hand between her legs and slipped his fingers beneath her thong.

"Your pussy *is* wet, Milady."

She shook her head and he laughed. It was a satisfied, rather than triumphant sound.

"Shall I finish you off?" he asked, pressing a thumb to her swollen clit.

"I…"

"It's just you and me. I'll keep your secret. No one will have to know."

She wanted to refuse, should refuse. But she'd never known desire this debilitating. Even if she found someone else or went somewhere to satisfy herself, it wouldn't be the same. She needed *him*.

He made maddening circles on her clit, and he had one finger teasing her entrance.

"Do it," she instructed.

"Ask."

Damien was making it clear he was in charge, not her. No doubt he'd give her what she wanted, but her compliance would be the cost. "Yes," she said. "I'd like an orgasm."

When he didn't change the tempo, she closed her eyes. He allowed her the time and the space to wage her internal battle. Sensations assailed her, forcing her body to relax. She became a puddle of feminine hunger. "Please," she whispered.

"Look at me."

She did.

"Ask again."

She understood. He wouldn't let her escape or pretend she hadn't been aware of what she was doing. "Please, Damien. Give me an orgasm."

"My pleasure, Milady."

He circled her clit and inserted two fingers deep inside her pussy. He finger-fucked her as he teased her clit.

Her legs shook with the force of his movements.

There was nothing sweet about this, and it was beyond hot. "Damien." This man was watching her reactions and responding to them.

"Come for me, Catrina."

He pressed his fingers against her G-spot.

Mindless of her surroundings, she screamed as the climax crashed into her. He helped her ride it, keeping his grip tight on her wrists, pressing her against the wall, supporting her body.

"So, so perfect," he said.

She screamed a second time, shattered. Her body went limp, but she wasn't worried, he was there, holding her in a firm but tender grip.

It seemed like minutes later when she blinked and looked at him.

"Welcome back," he said.

"That was…" She held back the words, desperate to be on firm footing again.

"For me, too."

"I'm not sure I understand."

"I adore a woman who is so responsive. I appreciate you playing with me." He moved his hand from between her legs and straightened her thong and skirt.

She pulled her wrists free from his grip. "It changes nothing."

"Maybe not for you. It makes me want to know you more."

"Do you always use sweet words to make all the women swoon, Damien?"

"That was a scene, and you know it. This is different."

"Is it?"

He took her hand and placed it on his crotch. "You tell me."

"So? You have a hard-on."

"Were you born a cynic?"

She shook her head. "Life taught me."

"I can teach you other things, show you a different perspective. You'll be a better Domme for the experience."

"You did that to prove something to me?"

"Partially."

She wasn't sure if she was hurt or shocked or pissed. "At least you're honest." She put up a hand to push him away.

"The truth is, I did that because I wanted to get you off, because I'm attracted to you."

Just because he sounded sincere, didn't mean he was.

"Give me two weeks," Damien said.

"What?"

"I'm challenging you. Spend two weeks with me, submit to me, see if the experience transforms you."

"Not just no, but hell no."

"What are you scared of?"

"Nothing scares me." Another lie. Plenty scared her, and with good reason.

"Then agree to it. You've got nothing to lose. You'll experience new things, get to spend a few days up here, have a chance to relax in a way you never have."

"Relax?" she scoffed.

"What would it be like if you could be yourself and let go, turn over control to someone else for a while?"

"I can't," she said, her heart thundering. That was as honest as she'd been with anyone, ever.

He inclined his head, showing he'd heard the fear in her voice. *Damn him.*

"Was it scary when I brought you off?"

She shook her head.

"When I made you ask for it?"

"No."

A woman on her way to the locker room walked past without disturbing them.

"I will demolish your barriers, Catrina."

A traitorous part of her wanted to say yes. Instead, she met his gaze. His eyes were dark, probing. She was afraid he saw too much.

He brushed a strand of hair back from her face.

She had to go before her resolve crumpled. "Thanks for the orgasm. My shuttle will be here soon."

He moved aside. As she walked past, he swatted her, catching the bare flesh above her stockings and below her buttocks.

Shock stole her breath. She stopped and rounded on him. Before she could speak, Damien had her against the wall, overwhelming her with his scent, his presence.

The sting receded, leaving a tantalizing warmth that stunned her and made it impossible to string coherent thoughts together. Despite herself, she grabbed his shoulders and held on tight.

He leaned forward and kissed her forehead before moving lower to graze her neck.

His gentleness surprised her, obliterating her defenses.

"Be at my place in Denver tomorrow night at eight," he whispered in her ear. "Just the two of us, Catrina."

"You know I can't."

"If two weeks is too frightening, start with one night. Eight o'clock," he repeated. "Be there."

Chapter Two

"You're out of your mind," Catrina told him. And the fact she was still hanging onto him proved that she was out of hers, too.

"Am I? Or am I offering what you secretly want?"

She maneuvered her hands to push him away. Budging him, she found out, was something that required his cooperation. Big, intractable men were another reason she liked being a Domme. "Move," she instructed.

"You're bossy."

"I'm assertive," she corrected. "Don't you forget it, mister."

With a smile capable of making her forget her resolve, Damien stepped back. Trying to think rationally, she escaped.

Gregorio was in the foyer, his arms crossed as usual.

"I've got to get out of here."

He gave a sharp nod. "Of course."

After what seemed like hours, he returned with her coat and small handbag.

"I couldn't find the hatcheck girl," he admitted. "So it took me a minute."

Tension continued to tighten her stomach.

Then Damien—damn him—reappeared at her side. He plucked her coat from her Gregorio's grip.

"I don't need your help," she insisted.

"Regardless, you've got it." He moved behind her.

Deciding not to struggle with him, she shrugged into her coat.

"That wasn't so bad, was it?"

"Thank you," she said, looking at him. "I've got it from here."

He held up a hand. "I'm being prudent. It's snowing, and your boots aren't made for the ice."

"Does everyone get this kind of personal service from the owner?"

"Of course not."

She met his gaze. His intense blue eyes seared her.

"It's okay to accept help, Milady."

For her, it wasn't. She'd been doing things on her own for so long that she wasn't certain she knew how else to behave.

"Think of me as your willing servant, if it helps."

"Right," she agreed.

Even Damien's lips twitched at the ridiculousness of the suggestion.

Gregorio opened the front door and said goodnight to a couple who were heading out.

"Well?" Damien asked.

She didn't need any assistance. But she knew that he wouldn't be dissuaded. Since she had no intention of seeing him privately, she reasoned that giving in here just avoided a scene. "Thank you," she said, placing a hand on his forearm.

Immediately she recognized her error. Nothing was harmless with this man. Heat and strength radiated from him and through her. His effortless way of making her feel insulated and taken care of was both irresistibly sexy and unbelievably dangerous.

Gregorio opened the door for them. Bitter cold air nipped at her ears and she shivered.

"You're welcome to stay," Damien invited.

"No chance."

Outside, the atmosphere hung heavy with humidity. Dozens of lights outlined the flagstone path. Silence shrouded them, and for a moment she could believe they were the only two people on the planet.

Despite his dire warnings, the way had been shoveled, and a layer of salt had been thrown down, providing traction and melting the occasional snowflakes as they landed. "You'll say anything to get your way, won't you?"

"I'll say anything to spend a few extra minutes with you," he corrected.

He helped her into the backseat of the oversized and luxurious four-wheel-drive vehicle that served as the shuttle. Fortunately, she was the only occupant.

"Take good care of her, Jeff," Damien instructed the driver. He reached across her lap and fastened her safety belt.

"Of course, sir."

Damien slid his thumb across the back of her hand.

A shiver that had nothing to do with the temperature danced up her spine.

"Tomorrow," he reminded her.

Before she could respond, he closed the door.

As the driver pulled away, she glanced over to see Damien give her a little salute. He continued toward the porch, brushing snowflakes from his hair.

"You must be important to the boss," Jeff said, meeting her gaze in the rearview mirror.

"Not at all."

The man chuckled. "This could be fun to watch."

"Fun?"

"The boss doesn't like to be told no."

"He's going to hear it a lot from me," she replied.

"That's why it will be fun to watch."

She couldn't help herself. His enthusiasm was infectious and she grinned.

He stopped at the intersection with the highway. "Are you at the Lodge?"

"Promise not to tell Damien?"

"As if he wouldn't find out anyway, Milady."

"I'm sure you're right." Not that Damien cared enough to track her down, she was sure. "The Lodge," she confirmed.

Jeff lapsed into silence. Why couldn't all men be like him? Big, rugged, quiet and happy to leave her the hell alone?

Though she collapsed against the luxurious leather, she couldn't relax. Damien's words played over and over in her mind.

For years, she had told herself that she would never submit to anyone. So that went double for a Dom amongst Doms.

But damn... Even though they were now separated by miles, every breath she took smelled of him. Her body seemed seared from his quick spank.

Her cell phone rang.

"That will be the boss," Jeff said.

She dug the device from her purse and checked the display.

"I was right, wasn't I?"

Catrina ignored the call.

"You're trying to delay the inevitable," Jeff said.

The phone rang again.

"Sorry, Milady. I warned you. You matter to the boss."

With a deep sigh, she answered the call.

"I can't stop thinking about you," Damien said by way of a greeting.

The sound of his voice sent sparks of remembrance straight to her scorched skin. She knew it was impossible that the area would still be marked, but the psychic imprint from his touch remained. "I haven't thought about you once," she said.

He laughed. "Do you know how to tell the truth? Once you're at your hotel, you'll take a shower and masturbate."

"No," she insisted, the word breathless, hurried.

"I should forbid it," he said.

"As if I'd do what you told me to."

"Well isn't that a conundrum? If you touch yourself, you'll imagine it's my fingers tracing your skin. If you don't play with that pretty pussy, you'll be following my explicit command. Oh, and, Milady…"

Keenly aware of Jeff's interest, she remained silent.

"Lick your fingers when you're done," Damien finished.

Without another word, the damnable man hung up.

It wasn't until a few seconds later that she realized Jeff had parked beneath the hotel's portico. He opened her door and escorted her to the entrance despite her protests.

"When the boss issues an order, *I* follow it," he said.

"Are you insinuating I should do likewise?"

"Oh, hell no. It's much more fun this way." He waited until she was inside before making a dash back to the sports utility vehicle.

In her room, she dropped her coat on the end of the bed. She sat on a chair to remove the tight-fitting boots. The cursed things might be gorgeous, but they hurt like hell. It felt as if her toes would be cramped for days.

During their time together, Damien had turned her inside out. And if he had his way, they'd continue their exploration tomorrow.

She stripped and folded her clothes then placed them in her suitcase to make packing easier. Afterwards, she headed for the bathroom to scrub off her make-up. No doubt the plain and ordinary Catrina would appeal to him a lot less than the dramatic diva she portrayed.

But she couldn't help but wonder what he was like away from the Den.

Catrina turned on the shower faucet. As steam billowed in the room, his earlier words haunted her. The damnable man *had* created a conundrum.

She was aroused, and she didn't want to be.

Gritting her teeth, she entered the stall.

As he'd hoped, her thoughts were filled with images of him. She didn't want to play with him. And she most certainly had no intention of submitting to him.

But as she closed her eyes, she recalled the stunning shock that had rocked her when his hand had connected with her flesh.

The momentary hiss of pain had been replaced almost immediately with the white-hot heat of desire, making all her protests irrelevant.

Warmth from the water suffused her. Focusing on her shower, she opened her eyes and reached for the bar of soap then made a lather. She slid her slick hands over her chest. Her nipples beaded, and her breasts were swollen.

Damn him.

With her lips pursed, she continued down her belly. She paused for a moment at her pelvis. Her pussy ached from a lack of fulfilment.

No matter how she justified things or what stories she told herself, the truth was, she didn't have sex as often as she would have liked. All too often she used her trusty vibrator. And the idea of having Damien's cock inside her made her tremble.

Lightly, she skimmed her fingers across her pussy before continuing on. No doubt she would survive, even without an orgasm.

She finished up then dried off.

Sleep remained elusive. She checked the time every five to ten minutes, until she became so frustrated that she tossed a pillow on top of the offending clock to block out the mocking numbers.

Around eight, three hours later than she usually slept, she finally gave up the battle and threw back the sheets.

A text message from Damien was waiting on her phone.

I hope you didn't steal an orgasm that belongs to me.

Her heart thundered. *Belonged to him?* How arrogant could the man be? But if she were honest with herself, she'd admit the words sent a little thrill through her.

The words were part of the reason he was such a good Dom. If he behaved this way with everyone, that meant he started the seduction, the alluring mind-fuck, hours before he'd ever touched his submissive. Maybe she could learn a thing or two from him. Not that she'd ever admit that to him.

Still, she hadn't decided how to respond when a second text followed.

If you're a good girl, you'll be rewarded.

Ignoring both messages, she dressed and rode the elevator to the lobby for a much-needed caffeine fix. Unfortunately, the tall, black coffee didn't help. In fact, it flooded her system with nerves. The combination of that and no sleep caused her to be jittery.

Then her phone vibrated, indicating he'd contacted her again, and that made things worse.

She looked at the screen. An address appeared on the display. If her guess was right, it was in a sprawling north-western Denver suburb, not too far from the foothills. Lots of land to go with the privacy and mountain views.

Catrina slammed the phone on the table, facedown.

Damn him for tempting her.

Preferring carbs over healthy eating, she ordered a waffle and slathered it in butter and maple syrup.

A number of people wandered into the dining room. She recognized some from the Den. Bradley and Master Lawrence strolled in, smiling at each other. They never looked in her direction. It had been a long time since she'd felt so alone.

Catrina paid her bill then went upstairs to finish packing before heading back to Denver.

With the snow-covered mountain roads, the drive took an hour longer than it usually did. And that gave her far too much time to think.

At her small but cozy Washington Park bungalow, she put away her clean clothing and tossed a load of laundry in the washing machine before going about her weekly chores. Even after she was finished, there were still too many hours left before she could go to bed.

She wandered into her office. She'd finished her monthly newsletter before heading to the Den, but she opened the document on her computer and proofed it a final time. Then she pulled out manila file folders belonging to women she was meeting with the next day. Her first appointment would be with her newest client, Lara. The woman's husband had stunned her less than a week ago with the news that he was filing for a divorce. In the twenty-eight years the couple had been married, Lara had allowed him to handle the bills and investing. When Catrina had met with her last week, Lara had cried the whole time.

At times, Catrina felt as if her role was one of a counsellor more than a financial advisor, but that was the part of the job, and she treasured it.

It had only been five years since she'd been in similar circumstances...facing the unexpected and unwelcome end of an intimate relationship and staring at the all-too-real possibility of financial ruin. Helping others navigate treacherous waters gave her life meaning.

An hour later, she closed the files and slid them back in the desk drawer.

She was sitting at her desk, staring out of the window at a couple walking past, holding hands, when angst returned in a massive rush.

The rest of the afternoon and evening loomed. She'd worked out before going to the Den, and she hated to overdo the exercise since she had a yoga class tomorrow after work. She didn't want to sit in front of the television all night, though that was becoming a bigger possibility with each passing minute.

She shoved her chair back from her desk and paced the hardwood floor of her still-to-be renovated home.

No light blinked on her phone, meaning Damien hadn't contacted her again. He obviously expected her to answer his summons, something she had little intention of doing.

An hour later, she wasn't as sure.

No matter what she focused on, she couldn't banish thoughts of him. Despite her resolve, he intrigued her.

Then her great internal debate began.

It couldn't hurt to see him.

But no good could come of it.

She wasn't a sub.

But she did like to learn and grow.

Since she hadn't masturbated, sexual tension crawled through her. She hadn't deliberately followed his orders, yet she ached to feel his strong hands on her body.

Damn it. She didn't need his touch. She needed someone's. *Anyone's.*

No matter how hard she tried to convince herself she didn't need the devastating Dom, she couldn't banish his image from her mind.

Cursing her traitorous thoughts, she set up the coffee pot for the next morning and programmed its timer. It wasn't even five o'clock in the afternoon.

One thing was certain, she needed an outlet for her turmoil.

She telephoned a couple of friends—no one was available to hang out.

As a desperate measure she called Bradley. He begged off with an apology, saying he had to get ready for work the next day, adding in a sheepish voice that Master Lawrence had exhausted him.

That left only one option.

With confidence, she dialed her mother's number. Evelyn didn't answer until the fourth ring. With a gleeful giggle, she said she was going to a movie with a new beau.

Her mother had plans? Then it hit her. "Wait. What? When did you get a boyfriend?"

"A few weeks ago. Milton. He likes to rock climb at an indoor gym. Can you imagine?"

"I'm having a hard time getting past the fact you're dating, Mother."

"Yeah. Isn't it cool?"

"Cool?" She pulled the phone away from her ear and looked at it. "Sorry, who is this? I thought I was talking to my mom."

"I've got to go. Miltey will be here in a few minutes, and I hate to keep him waiting."

Miltey? In the background, Catrina heard the sound of her mother's doorbell.

"I'm sure you'll find something to do, dear. Give me a call later this week. Maybe you can meet him."

Her mother hung up without a formal goodbye.

At times like this, that nasty, nasty internal voice turned up the volume, reminding Catrina she'd made the choice to shut herself off from intimacy and that there were consequences for it. She informed her clients it was okay to trust again, even fall in love, as long as they made savvy financial decisions and didn't abdicate all their power. But she hadn't been able to take her own advice.

The clock on the kitchen wall indicated it was a few minutes past seven. She still had time to make it to Damien's house.

Catrina raked a handful of hair back from her forehead.

Who was she fooling? A man hadn't held her interest like this in years, if ever. In fighting herself and him, she was also fighting the inevitable. She could see him again and prove to herself that last night had been an anomaly. And she could collect a fabulous, well-earned orgasm.

* * * *

Damien prided himself on the fact that nothing rattled him.

He owned half a dozen businesses and executed transactions in a handful of different time zones. Others came to him to solve their problems.

So why the hell was he wearing a path in the living room's hardwood floor?

Annoyed with himself, he checked his watch. Until this moment, he'd had no doubt Catrina would show up.

He'd expected her to be a few minutes late, but twenty?

Half an hour ago, he'd flipped the switch to ignite the fireplace, bumped the house temperature a couple of degrees, turned on the porch and path lights then uncorked a bottle of wine.

Afterwards, instead of staring out of the window, he'd forced himself to return to his study to finish up an email to a potential client in Hong Kong. That had taken all of three minutes.

He'd flipped the lid closed on his notebook computer then tried to settle on the couch.

After Catrina had left the Den last night, he'd been restless. A little after two o'clock, Gregorio had locked up and headed for his own quarters.

For the first time since his divorce a decade before, Damien had noticed how large his suite was, how big and empty his house was.

He'd ached to hold Catrina in his arms. Not just any woman. Catrina, specifically. There was something about her scent, the way she fought him, the way her eyes — the color of crushed emeralds — glittered when she challenged him. And more, it was the way she tried to hide her vulnerabilities.

This morning, Gregorio had joined him for coffee and breakfast, and the two had spent most of the day in meetings. But Damien had been distracted by thoughts of the lovely Domme. Damien knew he was a fortunate man. Over the years, he'd interacted with a number of subs, so many that he'd become jaded, enough that he was rarely tempted to scene anymore. Maybe that was why the attraction to Catrina intrigued him.

At the Den, he'd been aware of her scrutiny as he'd led the demonstration with Susan.

When Catrina had vanished from the room before the presentation had ended, he'd suspected she'd been turned on by what she'd witnessed. The dampness of her pussy had confirmed his suspicions. She'd been aroused, even though she hadn't wanted to be.

Ever since, he'd been tormented by thoughts of her, recalling her scent and her soft, feminine sounds of pleasure and pain. He wanted to hear more, wanted to feel her pussy clenching his cock, wanted to inhale the scent of her hair when the luxurious strands spilled across his chest.

Damien hadn't been surprised when she'd ignored his text messages. That she hadn't told him to fuck off meant she was interested. That she hadn't replied meant she was conflicted.

He'd figured she'd show up five to ten minutes late, making it clear she wouldn't willingly fall at his feet. Fifteen had made him question his tactics. Twenty had made him nervous.

Now, as she edged toward twenty-five, anxiousness gnawed at his insides. As a rule, he didn't let relationship issues bother him. Women wanted to play or they didn't, and either way, he was fine with it.

Or at least he had been until this dark-haired beauty had ensnared his attention.

Out of the window, he saw the unmistakable beam of headlights as a car turned into his cul-de-sac. He watched, arms folded, as the vehicle pulled to a stop in front of his home.

More relieved than he would ever admit, he exhaled before closing the blinds to insure their privacy.

He opened the front door and leaned against the jamb, comfortable despite the chill that promised snow. With practiced patience, he waited for her even though she took her time turning off the car engine. He wanted her to come to him of her own volition. Nothing else would do.

She exited the sedan then hesitated for a moment when she saw him. He inclined his head in greeting, though he wasn't sure she would notice his expression across the distance.

She turned up the collar on her coat before grabbing her purse and flicking the car door closed. Purposefully, she walked up the path...toward him.

"I'm glad you came," he said, stepping aside to allow her to enter.

"I wasn't sure I was going to."

"Why did you?"

As she passed him, he caught a whiff of her just-showered scent, something tropical that reminded him of summer. Her hair was piled atop her head, with some sort of stick in it. He was sure the carved, green glossy piece had a fancy name, but damned if he knew what it was. No matter how much time he spent around women, some things they did remained a wonderful, alluring mystery.

He closed the door behind her.

"I don't know," she admitted. "Curiosity, maybe."

"You've bruised my ego."

She looked at him and seemed to be trying not to smile. "You were imagining I was so overcome by last night's orgasm that I spent the last eighteen hours fantasizing about you?"

"A man can hope."

"Dreamer."

He grinned. "May I take your coat?"

After interminable seconds, she placed her purse on a nearby table.

He moved behind her and helped her from the full-length garment then hung it in the closet.

When he'd imagined her coming to his home, he hadn't known what to expect. Would she dress as a fierce and fiery Domme? Or would she wear a skirt that invited him to touch her?

But, as he was starting to learn, this woman was not predictable.

Damien loved seeing her at the Den with her dramatic make-up, false eyelashes and bright lipstick. But this...? Other than a light brush of mascara, her face was bare.

Black jeans rode low on her hips, and a form-fitting sweater showed off her slender waist and the curve of her breasts. Instead of stilettos, she'd selected boots with chunky heels and metal buckles. Tonight she looked more like a biker chick than a Domme fatale.

She sure as hell didn't look ready to submit.

Just how many facets were there to this woman? One thing was certain. He fucking itched to find out. "Wine?" he offered.

"I'm driving."

"You're welcome to stay the night rather than go back out in the cold."

"Do you have a guest room?"

"Battered," he replied.

"Battered?"

"My ego. Turns out it's not just bruised, it's battered."

She smiled. This time, it was genuine, not polite like the ones she used at the Den. It was then that he realized how much of herself she kept hidden. The more he saw, the more he wanted to learn.

"I'll have a glass of wine. No more than one," she clarified as she followed him into the kitchen.

He poured a small amount in her glass.

She swirled it around then tasted it and said, "Nice."

"I'm glad you approve. It's one of my favorites," he agreed. He filled his glass while she wandered toward the sliding patio door.

She moved aside the blinds to look outside. "Is that Standley Lake out there?"

"It is."

"I had no idea it was so big."

"Plenty of water skiing in summer."

"So you have a view of the mountains and the water?"

"Depending on the angle. And a covered patio," he said. "It will be chilly, but we can have coffee out there in the morning. A pair of bald eagles breeds here."

She released the blinds and they swished into place as she turned to face him. A scowl was buried between her eyebrows. "You keep assuming I'm staying."

"Not at all. Just sweetening the offer."

"Do you always get your own way?"

"By any means, fair or foul."

Catrina shook her head. "You're honest."

"To a fault." He crossed to her and skimmed a finger down her cheekbone. "I like to touch you," he said. "Last night showed me how much."

She captured his wrist.

"You like it, too. I can see your heart beating, right there…" He continued lower, tracing the column of her throat.

Her breath caught.

"And the rise and fall of your chest tells me you're affected, too." He spread his hand on her sweater, above her breasts.

Catrina was a tall woman, but she barely reached his chin. He wanted to wrap her up and keep her safe from the things that scared her.

She moved his hand aside then put some distance between them. "Your place isn't what I expected. I figured you more for an executive loft downtown." She rested her hips against a countertop. "Oh, no. Wait. I was wrong. This suits you fine."

"You're talking fast, Catrina." But he gave her the space she seemed to need. He pulled out a barstool and sat on it. She was here. That was enough.

"You've got tons of privacy. Your subs can scream all they want without disturbing the neighbors. Why don't you lead the way?"

"I beg your pardon?"

"To your dungeon? Didn't you invite me here to get me naked and prove how susceptible I am to your charms?"

"Are you trying to piss me off?"

She blinked.

He placed his wine glass on the quartz. "Maybe you're annoyed with yourself because I tempt you, or that you're curious. Perhaps you crave a taste of leather on your butt cheeks and don't know how to ask for it."

"You're ridiculous." She gripped the stem of her glass with two hands.

"If you want to be over my lap, I'd be delighted to accommodate you. But you can't make it easy, can you? If you'd worn something more appropriate, I'd know you wanted to feel us, bare skin to bare skin. Instead you're lying to me. And worse, to yourself." He moved his glass aside. "So answer my earlier question, Catrina. Why did you come?"

"Nothing better to do."

He nodded. "I believe that."

She relaxed her hold a bit.

"But there's more."

She shook her head.

"Do you ever demand honesty from your subs?"

"I'm not sure what you're asking."

"I understand why I terrify you."

"You don't," she contradicted.

"Oh, I do." He stood and pushed back the wooden stool. "You're not afraid of the sexual aspect at all. In fact, you'd be happy to play with me as long as I just spanked your ass and got you off."

Her lips parted and she stood there, as if riveted.

"But you know I'm going to demand more from you than you want to give."

"Not true," she protested.

"Really?" He took a few steps toward her. To her credit, she straightened her shoulders. "I won't be satisfied with a few minutes together. I don't want to show you to my dungeon and force you to your knees, though at the moment, the idea does have some merit."

She flinched.

"That might send you scurrying, but it wouldn't frighten you. What terrifies you, though, is the idea that I want to get to know you. I want to know what keeps you awake at night, why you're scared of having something that isn't shallow."

"Don't give up your day job," she replied. "You suck as a psychiatrist."

"Why do you need men to lick your boots?"

She rolled her eyes. "I like it. Why do you need to women to be subservient?"

"I don't, and they're not. Women are my equal."

"Please. I watched the demo you did with Susan."

"Then you noticed the way I looked at her, watching all of her reactions. You would have also been aware that everything I did was solely to meet her needs. Just as I met yours last night."

Catrina took a sip from her wine. He imagined she did it to appear nonchalant, but the way the wine splashed indicated her hand was shaking.

"Just as I will meet them again tonight." He moved in closer and plucked her glass from her hand. "Admit it" —he slid her glass onto the countertop—"a BDSM relationship is about way more than getting your sexual kink on. It's about an exchange of energy, about being so focused on another person that their happiness becomes paramount to you. Your sub's fulfilment matters more than your own."

"I get my subs off."

"Before or after they pleasure you?"

She looked away.

"I'm not criticizing you," he said. "Merely suggesting there's more to it than you realize."

She met his gaze.

"Have you masturbated?"

"What kind of question is that?" she asked, her voice sounding delightfully breathless.

Damien knew how seductive the right sexual partner could be. That's why having her here meant something to him. "Since you didn't respond to my earlier text, I'm curious to know whether or not you followed my instruction."

"No." Then she clarified, "I didn't touch myself."

"I promised you a reward if you were good."

She swallowed deeply. Then she looked up at him. He felt as if everything he knew about subs vanished. Each was unique in her needs and experiences, but Catrina, with her sudden shiver and wide, unblinking eyes was going to be a challenge...one he was looking forward to.

"Milady, if you'd wanted to hang out, you would have invited me to meet you for dinner or a coffee, but you didn't. So I'll make this easier for you. Shall I order you to strip? Or would you like to do it of your own free will?"

Chapter Three

Why the hell did this man need to make things so difficult? It annoyed her to think he knew her as well as she knew herself. Maybe even better. She'd spent the past five years protecting herself. Damien, though, kept pushing. He recognized that she kept dodging his questions, and he circled back to them until she answered.

"Here," he said. "Now."

Her pulse stalled, and she could hardly think straight. She'd never done this for a man. She set the scene, named the time and place and she was dressed for play when her boys arrived.

Before she'd become a Domme, she'd typically changed into a robe in the bathroom, then met her date in the bedroom. Standing in a man's kitchen and peeling off her clothes wasn't something she'd ever done before.

Damien confused her. This wasn't a seduction, and he hadn't taken her to his dungeon, nor had he laid out any toys.

Except for what had already happened between them and the fact he'd told her to get naked in his kitchen, she could believe they were on a first date getting ready to go to dinner.

"You're not shy, are you?" he asked. When she didn't respond, he gentled his voice and said, "I would have never suspected. Take your time. But I will have you nude. Would you like some help?"

"Uhm..."

He made the decision for her. He took hold of her sweater, tugged it from her waistband and pulled it up and over her head with a single, smooth move. Part of her hair dislodged and fell over her forehead and down her face.

She forced herself to breathe.

He stepped back, giving her some space, but not much. This man knew what he was doing.

He draped her sweater over the oven door's handle and stood there, regarding her.

She crouched to remove her boots and socks, and he offered a steadying hand.

Though she was tall, she felt tiny standing before him in bare feet. She'd had no idea how unnerving this could be.

Before she could lose her courage, she removed her jeans.

He picked them up from the hardwood floor. As she shimmied out of her underwear, he folded her pants.

He extended his hand for her thong.

Wordlessly, she shoved the skimpy piece of cotton against his palm.

"You're beautiful, Catrina."

She noticed that he'd stopped calling her Milady. Subtly, inexorably, he asserted his power.

Then he nodded. Understanding, she unhooked her bra and shucked the straps from her shoulders.

"Thank you," he said, accepting the lingerie.

Catrina resisted the impulse to cover up. Instead, she drew her shoulders closer together.

"I turned up the heat before you arrived. Let me know if you're cold. Have you ever knelt for a man?"

"No."

He switched topics faster than anyone she'd ever known. It kept her off balance and from dwelling on anything for too long.

"I'm not about to start now."

"I can't and won't compel you to do anything. I respect everything you say and all your wishes."

His rich voice, thick and warm like whiskey warmed near a fire, hypnotized her.

"We can and should talk about anything that makes you uncomfortable. You may use the Den's safe word or one of your own."

"Halt is fine." Since the words emerged squeaky, she cleared her throat and tried again.

He nodded. "It would give me great pleasure to see you kneel for me. You may use the rug."

As each moment passed, she fell deeper under his spell. At the Den and other places she'd played, she had watched submissives lower themselves with great care and elegance. She'd also seen some newer subs struggle with it. Part of her couldn't believe she was even considering it. "I thought this was about my pleasure?"

"It is."

She scowled. She appreciated that he didn't tell her to trust him or turn it into a debate—he said his piece then shut up.

Damien once again offered his assistance. Using his forearm for balance, she went to her knees, grateful for the thickness of the rug. Subs knelt for her all the time, and she'd never given much consideration to the surface. She knew she should be grateful for his foresight.

"How is it?"

She cricked her neck to look at him. "I really, really hate it."

"Then get up."

"What?" she snapped.

"I meant it when I said I won't force you to do anything."

"But…"

"If you want to stop, do so." He folded his arms in his usual manner.

She remained where she was.

"What do you hate about it?"

"It hurts my neck."

"Fair enough. Anything else?"

"It's subservient."

"If you want to look at it that way."

She exhaled, not sure why she was still on her knees. But him talking to her, rather than walking away, made it possible. "What other possible way is there?"

"You tell me."

"Has anyone ever told you how frustrating you are?"

"Once or twice, perhaps." A tiny smile ghosted his lips.

This side of him, light, jovial, was endearing. Her self-consciousness was ebbing. Because he treated it as if it were natural, it seemed that way.

This was different from the way she interacted with her boys. They showed up ready to play and she accommodated their desires. Before each one's arrival, she set the scene, getting out her toys, arranging them, and when they walked through the door, she took charge right away. Damien had as well, but with his unique flair. He was gentler than she'd mentally planned for. A harder-edged Damien would have brought out a similar response in her. Instead, she found her defenses crumbling.

He waited.

She drank in his silent strength. He stood with his denim-clad legs slightly apart. The leather on his boots was well-worn, and his belt looked supple, as if it were an old friend. He wore a short-sleeved, dark T-shirt that showed off his biceps. His muscular build was so damn sexy.

Sometimes he pulled back his longish hair and secured it, but tonight it was untamed, curling well below his nape.

She'd always thought of him as elegantly rough, but tonight, she saw a different side of him, patiently resolved.

After a full thirty seconds during which he said nothing, she answered, "You asked me to kneel to ease my nerves."

"You're a quick study." He captured that stray lock of her hair and tucked it behind her ear. "You were nervous. I wasn't expecting that, so I changed my approach. The longer I allowed you to think about things, the more you'd be tempted to run. But you needed time to get comfortable with me as well as yourself and the dynamic of your new role. I don't want you to overthink the moment. But there's more. I like to look at you. And yes, if you can relax enough to think about what I want and transcend your conflicting thoughts, you complying with my requests can bring us both pleasure."

He hadn't yet touched her in anything other than a casual way. There was no doubt he was earning her trust.

"When you're ready, I'd like you to sit on the peninsula." He pointed to the expanse of quartz with the barstools beneath it.

His request shocked her. Since he didn't appear to be joking, she rose and walked the short distance, aware of his gaze on her rear end.

She put her arms behind her and leveraged herself into position. Suddenly she wished she'd taken a gulp of her wine while she'd had the chance.

"You look more spectacular than I'd imagined."

"You thought this up in advance?" she asked, crossing her legs.

"Oh, yes."

"You're a wicked man."

"You have no idea, Milady. Please lie back and uncross your legs."

Catrina wrinkled her nose. "Are you planning what I think you're planning?"

"I hope so."

"I'm not sure about this."

"You can always refuse," he reminded her.

"No way."

"I didn't think you would."

"Don't gloat."

"Never, Milady."

Milady again. From him, it sounded more affectionate than a term of respect. But she didn't mind.

"You may be more comfortable if you remove that contraption from your hair."

She reached up, but halted when he asked, "May I?"

"Thank you."

He pulled out the chopstick and her hair tumbled around her shoulders and down her back. "Doesn't matter which way you wear it," he said, "it's fabulous." He smoothed it to one side. "Now let's get on with it."

The quartz slab beneath her bare body was firm and cool, a startling contrast to the heat chasing through her.

"This is your reward for honoring my request not to touch yourself. Though I might have enjoyed the idea of you sucking your juices from your fingers." He moved between her legs and parted her labia.

Though she squirmed, he didn't reprimand her. Nor did he command her to remain still.

When he placed his thumb against her clit, she lifted her hips scandalously.

"That's it," he said.

She wished she could see his expression, but he bent to lick her from back to front.

The pressure of his tongue nearly undid her. She cried out, already on the verge of climaxing.

"Come whenever you want."

It hadn't occurred to her that he might make her delay her orgasm. She oftentimes compelled her subs to wait, and Damien's words brutally reinforced the fact that, in coming here, she had ceded a certain amount of control to him.

All those thoughts vanished when he slid a finger inside her.

Desperately she dug her heels into cabinets beneath her as she tried to lift her hips even higher.

Her insides tightened and her juices flowed.

The combination of the way he simultaneously finger-fucked and ate her proved to be her undoing. "Damien!" She reached for his head and buried her hands in his hair.

In response to her urgings, he inserted a second finger inside her. She tried to sit up, or get away, anything.

He was wonderful and unyielding, licking her pussy, moving his fingers. This was a hell of a reward. She suddenly understood why Susan had looked at him with such awe. When you were the focus of Master Damien Lowell's attentions, you felt it. It was as if the rest of the world had been shut out.

She called out his name again as she tightened all her muscles in anticipation. Blood rushed in her ears.

This was...

Her thoughts fractured and she could no longer think.

An orgasm washed over her, its engulfing energy more potent than anything she'd ever experienced. Desperately gripping his hair, she screamed.

But Damien didn't stop.

"More," he said, his breath on her heated flesh.

"I... I can't." She meant it. The first had taken so much out of her, and she needed time to recover. That hadn't been a polite little climax—it had taken all she had. If he kept this up, she would just be uncomfortable.

"Stop fighting me." He flicked his tongue back and forth across her clit, faster and faster, ignoring her gasping protests.

Impossibly, a second orgasm began to churn inside her. She knew she wouldn't be able to find relief, but she couldn't force her mouth to work long enough to say anything other than his name.

He stretched her wider, overwhelming her. Then he reached up, twisted and squeezed one of her nipples.

The added sensation was enough, and she froze, unable to breathe.

He continued his relentless sensual assault, making her writhe from the exquisite combination of sensations, both pleasure and pain, until she spiraled into an abyss.

Time blurred.

She had no idea how long she lay there, but slowly she became aware that he'd removed his fingers and had stopped tormenting her clit.

When she opened her eyes, she saw him standing there, broad, tall, steady. He was fully dressed and she was splayed open before him, her labia swollen and exposed. Embarrassment made her lick her lips.

He helped her to sit up, then he removed his shirt.

She blinked. Did he want to fuck her on the countertop? "You can't be serious."

"I assure you I am." But one of those deadly smiles played at the corners of his mouth.

Surprising her, he put his shirt on her then untucked her hair. The black T-shirt enveloped her, and she snuggled into its warmth. The cotton was stamped by his scent, that of prestige and power, and she inhaled it deeply. She wouldn't tell him, but she had no intention of returning the garment to him.

"I need to keep you warm. I always take care of what's mine."

"I'm not yours," she protested.

"For now, you are. Get used to it. Warmer?"

"Thanks, yes."

His rugged handsomeness stole her breath. She'd wondered what he looked like, but the first glance of his bare chest exceeded her expectations. A smattering of hair arrowed downwards to disappear beneath the waistband of his jeans. She was tantalized, aching to touch him.

He eased her down to the floor and held her close.

Looking up at him, she said, "I suppose I should take care of you now. Give you a blowjob or something."

"I'm not done with you yet."

"Oh. Right. You need to tie me up before you fuck me or something equally diabolical."

"You can relax. I don't typically beat women until the second date." He snagged both glasses of wine.

Curious, she followed him into the living room and joined him on the couch that faced the fireplace. She tucked her legs beneath her and accepted the merlot. "This is an odd dungeon," she said.

"Building your anticipation."

"Uh, I'm good with never seeing it." Until tonight, she'd had no idea he had a sense of humor. That made her appreciate him all the more. "But I am puzzled as to what we're doing." What hot-blooded man wouldn't want to screw immediately after licking her cunt?

He faced her. "Talking."

"Talking?" With her being so exposed and his bare chest?

"That's the most important part of submission. The physical connection matters, but I'm considerably more interested in your brain than anything else."

"I'm not sure if you're being serious here."

"Very much. When you fully offer yourself to me, it will mean you've shared your emotions, your fears, vulnerabilities. Everything."

She laughed. "Good luck with that. That's what I have my girlfriends for. I don't do that with men."

"You prefer they keep their place, under your foot?"

"That sounds harsh."

"But true?"

She took a sip of her wine and allowed her hair to fall forward to hide her expression. As he had earlier, Damien brushed back the strands.

"I'd prefer you look at me when we talk."

She met his gaze and wished his eyes weren't that shocking shade of blue. He seemed to see into her, as if intent on prying out all her secrets. Despite the room's warmth, she shivered.

"When did you become a Domme? After a bad relationship?"

"So you became a Dom after a woman challenged you? You had to become a big, bad alpha male to prove something?"

Maddeningly, he kept his calm.

"I've always been a Dom," he responded, his voice as easy and well-modulated as it had been all evening. "There wasn't a moment or an event. It's not the same for you."

"What makes you all-knowing, all-seeing?" She scooted away from him. To his credit, he let her go.

"Because of the way you snapped at me just now."

"I didn't."

"I touched a nerve, Milady. I can live with that. In fact, I was hoping to do it. I meant it when I told you I want to know everything you've never shown anyone else."

"I was engaged," she said. "Until Joseph cleaned out the account we'd opened together." She tipped back her head. "We were saving for the wedding and for a house. Before he left, he maxed out my credit cards as well. And the worst thing about it…"

"Go on."

Damien hadn't tried to placate her or comfort her. He was simply listening.

"I freaking knew better," she finished. "Dad vanished before I was born, and my mother struggled her entire life, working two jobs to support us. I should have learnt from her, but I didn't. I fell in love and was goo-goo starry-eyed." She slid her glass onto the coffee table. "Once was enough."

"It seems like a leap from a guy being a dick to you being a Domme."

"I decided I would be in charge of my life, make my own decisions after that. I wanted to be equal in every way." Todd's words, though, haunted her. Had she bypassed equal and gone for control freak?

"All of your relationships have been casual since then?"

When she looked at him, he shrugged and added, "You've been coming to the Den for several years. I've rarely see you with the same sub."

"You're observant. There was one fairly serious relationship after my engagement ended," she confessed. "I..." She hesitated, choosing her words. "Todd was a nice guy, but boring, and so was the sex. So I took charge, and he took exception. Then I was at a party one day. My friend Joann had one too many margaritas and was entertaining everyone with the story. One of the guys there offered to kiss my feet. We all had a great laugh about it, but it turned out he'd meant it. He was a submissive, and he helped me explore my role. I took to it rather naturally."

"And now you want to accept my invitation to explore the dynamic from the other side."

"For one night. That's what we agreed." She said no more. He didn't need to know that after she'd left him, she'd been restless and filled with angst.

While she remained firm that she didn't want to trust a man again, she rationalized that she was simply playing with Damien. It didn't have to lead to anything serious. She was a grownup. They both knew the score. Why not have some fun?

"You're intrigued."

"Yes."

"Any other reason?"

She shook her head.

"How do you deal with one of your subs lying to you?"

Goosebumps chased up her arms. "I'm sorry?"

"It's a general question."

"My subs don't lie to me."

"Of course not. Your relationships aren't deep enough for that."

She opened her mouth to protest but closed it again. "That's a little unfair."

"Theoretically, then," he said. "What would you do?"

The conversation was making her squirm. "I don't know. Give him a spanking, maybe. Orgasm denial. Maybe a chastity device for a while." She grabbed a pillow and hugged it to her chest. "What's your approach?"

"First thing, I would try to find out the reason. Is she being a brat and hoping to get in trouble? Some subs crave a punishment as a way to feel cherished. Or is my beautiful sub scared? Maybe trying to protect her emotions? Has she been dishonest with herself for so long that she can no longer recognize the truth?"

He couldn't be talking to her, about her... Being with Damien was far scarier to her emotional health than she'd imagined.

"More than anything, I'd hope to establish the kind of relationship where my sub instinctively comes to me with issues and challenges. I'd want her to know I'd be there for her, that I was a rock in her life, someone she could turn to, no matter the crisis. After we figured out what was going on in a particular instance, I'd warn her that neither lies nor prevarication would be tolerated on that issue again, and we'd agree upon a punishment for any future infractions. I believe forthrightness is vital to a successful relationship."

"That's a nice hypothetical, Damien. You can have a scene with someone without having a relationship. You did with Susan last night."

"Agreed. But I see them as two different things. As a Domme, if you understand the complexities, you can make a scene richer, deeper, more compelling for your partner."

"I'm here, aren't I?"

"But you weren't entirely truthful with me earlier." He held up a hand when she started to protest. "Before we have an argument, let me tell you this. As I told you last night, when you're avoiding a question, you look down and to the left. If you have no need to protect yourself, you look me in the eye."

She didn't know whether it flattered or frightened her that his observation was so astute. Her mother had always known when Catrina was lying. Now she wondered if her mother had figured out the same thing Damien had. "We don't have a relationship, so I don't owe you anything."

"She said while looking me straight in the eye."

She blew out a breath. "You're insufferable."

"That was honest. So, would you like to answer, again, why are you here?"

"What I'd like is for you to mind your own business."

"When you're ready to tell me, I'll listen."

"Is this what you do to all your subs? Grind down their resistance so that they'll beg you to beat them just to get you to leave them alone?"

"You're onto something." Very deliberately, he put down his glass of wine.

Then, before she knew what was happening, he had her over his lap, her bottom upturned and exposed. The pillow went flying. She kicked and struggled and protested. He trapped her legs between his then delivered a sharp slap to her right buttock.

She froze.

"Have you ever had a spanking, Milady?"

"I thought you didn't beat a woman until the second date."

"You're the exception to almost all of my rules."

As much as she was able, she twisted to look at him. "I'm not sure what you think I've done to deserve this one. I thought you talked about punishments in terms of a negotiation."

"This, Milady, is not a punishment."

"Then what the hell do you call it?"

"Pleasure."

"You have a warped version of the word's meaning. That freaking hurt, and it sure as hell wasn't fun." She hadn't used a safe word, and she knew he had noticed, too.

"Oh?" He rubbed the affected area.

He caressed her buttocks with long, sweeping, repetitive strokes. Beneath his palms, her skin heated.

He ran his fingers up the insides of her thighs and tension eased from her body. Shocking her, she felt her pussy moisten. She remembered last night at the

Den, when he'd given her a smack. Her physical turn-on had been instant. If she had thought about it in advance, she would have expected to be angry that he'd touched her. Instead, the intensity had added to her pleasure.

"Still think it's not fun?"

"This is okay," she said.

"When you're ready for your spanking, let me know."

"You can massage all you want," she said.

"I hadn't figured you for a brat, Milady."

Was that how she was behaving? Trying to goad him into taking the decision away from her? The thought disturbed her.

"What do you want?"

"I'd like to get it over with," she said, her voice softer than usual.

"You want to be equal, Catrina. Tell me what to do."

She was lost in a spiral of confusion. She was aroused, wanting more, and it seemed a betrayal of her ideals to ask for it. Reminding herself she'd only agreed to one night and that she'd already learnt something, she said, "Spank me, Damien. Please." She tightened her buttocks in fear and anticipation, though she knew that oftentimes made pain worse.

He didn't tell her to relax. Instead, he helped her to do so with a light, gentle touch. On top of his earlier massage, this felt wonderful, making it impossible to hold onto any tension.

He started just above her knees and worked toward her buttocks. She became pliant. When he increased the force, she liked it. Earlier, he'd given her a smack that hurt, but this couldn't be more different. Though she found out what her subs liked and tried to deliver, being on the receiving end showed her, in a way that wasn't abstract, what it felt like. No wonder some of her executive playmates liked getting spanked. She felt her stress melt in the same way she did while meditating or working out.

"More?"

"Please."

When he continued she added, "Spank me harder, Damien."

He did, but gradually.

He took the time to finger her after giving her a dozen or so smacks. She used her toes as leverage to rise up, silently seeking more.

Damien didn't change what he was doing. She understood that he was delivering what she wanted, but at his pace, on his terms. Confounding Dom. But she had to admit, his way gave her a richer experience.

He varied the location, speed and impact of his hits.

"Surrender, Catrina."

She closed her eyes. The remaining parts of her hesitation were swept away as he continued the erotic dance on her flesh.

He teased her cunt and covered her legs and buttocks with blazing blows.

The more she went with it, the deeper she seemed to be swimming until an orgasm began to unfurl. She cried out his name, but the word emerged in a jumbled mess. She tried to move, but her legs felt lethargic.

"Do you want to come, Catrina?"

His voice seemed to come from quite a distance.

"Milady?"

"Yes," she whispered. "Yes. Please."

He drew moisture from her pussy and used it to insert a finger in her ass.

She whimpered.

He placed two more fingers in her heated core and moved in and out of both holes quickly, making it impossible for her to think. "Damien," she said.

"I've got you."

She expected him to ease up, but he didn't. Instead, he moved faster, purposefully. He grabbed a fistful of hair and pulled it, arching her head back. He kept her legs trapped. She was helpless, his prisoner.

Her body was stretched and arched, and she was aware of him everywhere, holding her still. Whatever he wanted to give or take, he could.

That she'd given him this much power made her shiver. She could take it back with a single word, and despite the temptation, remained silent.

Her stomach clenched at his persistent invasion. The feelings were almost too much, and she could barely breathe.

"That's it," he coached her. "Come for me, Milady." He pulled out his fingers, tugged her head back farther then re-entered her in a single, forceful push.

She screamed.

His ruthless domination shoved her over the edge into a stunning climax.

The orgasm made her go rigid. Time and space collided.

Moments later, she shuddered.

"Damn, you're responsive, Milady," he murmured, extracting his hand, turning her over and holding her against his chest.

Her first response was to push him away. She felt vulnerable and wanted to be alone. But when she started to move, he tightened his grip. He placed her head against his shoulder and stroked her hair, uttering soothing words that she couldn't quite make out.

He held her until her breathing evened out.

She'd never been held after lovemaking. Not that this scene had counted as lovemaking, she reminded herself. Then again, she'd never experienced anything quite like it. She'd gone from college sex, to an abbreviated engagement, to a ho-hum sexual encounter, to being a dominant. She gave comfort. She didn't receive it.

Damien kept his arms looped around her even when she straightened and put some distance between them.

"That was…" She tried to find words, but was lost when she looked at him.

Damien's eyebrows were drawn together over his electric blue eyes, and he said nothing. No one had ever regarded her as intensely.

He cocked his head to the side, indicating he'd wait as long as she needed.

"It was different than I thought it would be."

"In what way?"

Trying to steady herself, she drew a few breaths. "This sounds ridiculous."

"I doubt it."

"Humbled."

He nodded.

"But also empowered."

"Perfect," he said. "The dichotomy. The yin and yang of submission."

Though she'd had no real idea what to expect when he'd turned her over his knee, she hadn't been prepared for her emotions to be as overwhelmed as her body.

On some level it concerned her that he hadn't needed to cajole her compliance, rather, she'd offered it. "My ass really does sting," she said.

"Of course it does. It would hardly be a spanking if it didn't hurt."

That resolve-melting smile played around his mouth again.

Her heart warned her to run. He caught her chin. So much for thinking he'd allow her to hide.

"That was a hedonistic beating, meant to arouse both of us."

"I'm the only one who got off."

"Doesn't matter. I get fulfilment from turning you on. That's what it's about for me."

She looked at him.

"As a Dom, *your* Dom…when you come, I am pleased. Giving is more important than receiving."

Although her ideas of domination were similar to Damien's, the execution of their scenes were different. Before one of her boys arrived, she would chat with him on the phone. She would find out what he wanted, and they would discuss their mutual expectations. After a scene, she would soothe her sub, dry any of his tears, tell him how proud she was of him, allow him as much time as he needed to dress in street-legal clothes, but she didn't sit in patient silence for this long while he made sense of the physical experience. Maybe Damien was right. Maybe she did need to experience this for herself.

"How are you doing?"

She was shattered. No matter how much time he gave her, she wasn't sure she'd be able to comprehend the emotional implications of them being together. "I need to go," she said, pressing away from him.

Surprising her, he helped her up. "Let's get your clothes."

She made small talk while they went into the kitchen. "Remain there," he said. "Don't get dressed."

He excused himself and went into the bathroom, and she heard water running.

This was awkward, standing in the middle of the kitchen, half-naked. She supposed it shouldn't bother her as he'd eaten her while she was spread on his countertop. He had a way of demolishing her inhibitions.

A moment later, he returned with a damp cloth. "Spread your legs, Milady."

She knew better than to argue.

He crouched to bathe her pussy and ass. She appreciated the attention, but was becoming more and more desperate to make her escape. "Thank you," she said, when he nodded his satisfaction.

Aware of his gaze and wondering if her buttocks were bright red, she first pulled on her thong, then her jeans before tugging on her socks and stuffing her feet into her boots. She knew he noticed how much her hands trembled.

When she started to pull off his T-shirt, he said, "Keep it."

Back in the foyer, she gathered her discarded clothing, wadded it all up then shoved it into her purse. With a half-smile that felt as fragile as her control, she dug out her keys.

"I'll take those."

"Uh..."

"Milady, I'm not going to try to keep you here. I wish you would stay. And you're welcome to. But if you're intent on leaving, then I'll warm up your car while you finish getting dressed."

Put that way, how could she refuse, even if it prolonged the goodbye? She dropped the keys into his palm.

He pulled on a fleece jacket over his bare chest. Damn. No matter what he wore, he was a good-looking man. After turning up the collar, he headed outside.

Catrina shivered when she closed the door behind him. And it had nothing to do with the sudden gust of cold air that had swirled around her.

She heard the car engine start, and she shrugged into her coat before she could change her mind about leaving.

When he returned, a few snowflakes clung to his midnight-colored hair.

"I'll walk you out," he said.

Survival instinct warned her to run...now.

"Send me a text when you arrive home," he said.

"I'll be fine. The drive is short and the roads aren't all that—"

"Don't push your luck, Catrina." His words were tight with tension. He captured her chin and tipped back her head. "I didn't ask for a call. Just common courtesy. I'd prefer to tie you to the foot of my bed and keep you there until morning. So I think a text is a hell of a compromise."

She sucked in a breath. The image that kaleidoscoped through her mind terrified her. "You wouldn't do that."

"Of course not. That's far too uncivilized."

She exhaled.

"I'm not an ogre. I'd handcuff you to the headboard."

He gave her one of those wicked smiles that made it impossible to know whether or not he was joking.

"I need to go."

He walked her to the car. As she slid into the driver's seat, he leaned in and said, "You'll think about this interaction a lot. You'll relive it. And after you have, you'll be curious."

His voice wrapped around her, heating her.

"You'll wonder what else there is and what you're missing," he continued. "You liked the spanking. Maybe you didn't want to like it, or it offends your sensibilities that you enjoyed it. And we can talk about that. But the fact remains, you want more. You want me to fuck you as much as I want to be inside your hot pussy." He paused, but he didn't give her time to object. "You know my number. Call it anytime." Damien stepped back, started to close the door, but then hesitated. He captured a fistful of her hair, looped it around his hand to draw her head toward him, then finished with, "I meant it when I told you to text when you get home. If you don't, Catrina..."

She wanted to protest but couldn't find the words.

"I will give you a spanking you won't like and will always remember. Am I clear?"

She nodded.

"I didn't hear you," he said softly.

"Yes, Damien." She needed to escape while she still could, before she begged him to let her stay. Hell. He was right. As he spoke, a hundred different ideas tumbled through her brain, and it was as if she could already feel his cuffs around her wrists. "I understand," she said.

He pulled her head back a little more. Then he placed a light, gentle, full-of-promise kiss on her mouth before he released his grip.

"Drive safe, Milady."

Without another word, he closed the car door.

She pulled away, hands shaking, grateful she could drive without conscious thought. She looked in the rearview mirror. He remained where he was until she lost sight of him.

Chapter Four

Catrina clutched the steering wheel as she drove. The tension in her grip made her shoulders ache. Damien Lowell disturbed her in a way no other man ever had.

She'd been in love with her fiancé, or at least she thought she had been. In retrospect, she'd been thrilled with his attentions, enough that she'd ignored little things. The fact he was between jobs, and had been more than once. He'd always seemed to have some emergency. His car had broken down. Or he needed a new suit for a job interview. She'd paid his bills while telling herself that partners supported one another.

It shouldn't have shocked her when he'd taken off with all her money.

She'd learnt her lessons well, and she'd never allowed Todd to get past her exterior walls. He'd been a nice enough guy. She probably could have trusted him but had chosen not to.

And now…Damien.

He made her question everything she knew—or thought she knew—about relationships, and worse, about herself. Being a Domme gave her a huge sexual kick. And her partners enjoyed it as much as she did. But for her, it was more about staying in control.

What she'd just experienced with Damien had demolished that.

She'd enjoyed letting him take the lead. She'd liked the hot orgasm. And the spanking had aroused her. Afterwards, as she'd snuggled into his arms, it had been as if the outside world no longer existed. Her fears and worries had vanished.

When she'd been younger, more idealistic, she'd thought that it was possible for a man and woman to become partners and support each other. She'd been a romantic, even though she'd seen her mother's constant struggle for survival.

Tonight, he'd been supportive, wanting to know her inner thoughts and feelings. She'd glimpsed what it might be like to have someone to turn to. Part of her wanted to accept what he was offering.

She shook her head to clear it. Life had taught her to put away foolish, romantic notions. It might take all her resolve and determination, but she would do exactly that.

When she arrived at her cold, dark condominium, she sent a one-word text.

Safe.

She didn't want to get into a discussion or explain anything else.

Hearing his voice would undo her.

He'd told her she would want more, that she'd wonder what she was missing. And she was terrified to the tips of her toes that he might be right.

It was better to keep distance between them. Lots of it. Lots and lots of it.

* * * *

Confounding, frustrating, annoying-as-hell woman.

Damien shoved away from his computer at the Den. Damn it. He'd looked half a dozen times but he hadn't seen Catrina's name on the weekend's reservation list.

With a sigh, he strode to the window and stared at the expanse of pine trees and snow-covered ground.

It had been almost two weeks since she'd been to his house. As he'd requested, she had sent him a text that night, letting him know she'd made it home safe. Since then, he'd heard nothing from her.

He'd known the mini-scene had challenged her emotionally. *Fuck.* Who was he kidding? It had challenged him.

Her body language had indicated that she'd enjoyed what they'd done.

Perhaps a bit too sure of himself, he'd told her she'd want to explore further. But more, he'd hoped that they'd connected in a way she'd never imagined possible.

Their time together might have been short, but he'd held her. She'd told him about her fears and offered him a glimpse inside her carefully constructed defenses. There'd been no doubt she'd taken tentative steps toward trusting him.

She'd captivated him. He wanted the feeling to be mutual.

Because she'd let him in, he'd anticipated she might panic. He'd have been delighted, but surprised, if she had contacted him right away. He had expected her to take a couple of days to think things through, maybe as long as a week.

But this...? He was beginning to wonder if he'd misjudged the situation, and her.

"Boss?"

Damien looked over his shoulder. Gregorio stood in the doorway, scowling.

"I knocked twice," Gregorio said.

Turning, Damien waved the other man in. "Is the reservations system working correctly?"

"As far as I'm aware," Gregorio replied. "Are you having problems?"

Damien shook his head.

"Aha."

"Aha, what?" Damien asked. He spread his legs and folded his arms across his chest, matching Gregorio's stance.

"Things become clear."

"What the hell does that mean?"

"You drove up two weekends in a row. You're hoping to see someone specific."

"Don't you have work to do?"

"No. Really. Everything's set. I can listen to your woes for at least an hour."

"Out."

"You've got it bad."

"Are you hoping to get fired?"

"This is serious," Gregorio said. "If you're talking about sacking me and taking care of all of this yourself, you're not thinking straight. We need the good stuff."

"I might beat your ass."

"Would that help?"

Damien took a seat behind his desk. The two had been friends for years, and the question was sincere. Gregorio knew Damien's moods as well as Damien did. And if Damien needed the release, no doubt Gregorio would expose his back.

Without an invitation or permission, Gregorio crossed to a sideboard and opened a door. He slid aside a supposed-to-be secret panel and removed a crystal decanter of brandy. Of course, in typical fashion, the man had gone straight for Damien's private stash.

Gregorio removed the stopper then slowly poured a small amount into two separate snifters. He returned to slide one across the scarred desktop toward Damien.

"We've been through a lot," Gregorio said, taking a seat. "Relationship breakups..."

Including Gregorio's shocking divorce.

"Several new business ventures and one spectacular failure."

He didn't need reminding of that. Making the cover of a respected Wall Street newspaper because of a bankruptcy still gave him nightmares. No matter how many successes he'd had since, his portfolio had been tarnished.

"But I haven't seen you like this before."

"Like what?"

"Smitten," he clarified.

"Men don't get *smitten*."

"Fair enough. Obsessed. Mistress Catrina?"

"How —?"

"My brilliant deductive reasoning skills." Gregorio crossed his long legs. He grinned. "Susan was here last week with a new guy. You were cordial to them both. To my knowledge, you haven't played with anyone other than Mistress Catrina recently."

"No one should know about that."

"It's a small community, Boss. Someone saw you in the hallway with her. And the tension between the two of you when she left that night erased any doubt. And since she hasn't been back, I can't think of anyone else whose name you'd be looking for on the reservation system. Yep. There's no one else you'd be smitten by, well, I mean if you were smitten — which you're not — since men don't get smitten."

"Do you want to shut the fuck up now?"

"Oh, hell no. I'm just getting warmed up."

Gregorio grinned, pissing Damien off even more.

Damien breathed out, forcing himself to relax.

Contemplatively, he held his glass in his palm, warming the brandy. The ritual itself helped settle him.

A minute later, he brought the snifter closer and swirled again, releasing more of the alcohol's aroma. As always, he appreciated the sight of the liquid clinging mysteriously to the inside of the glass.

A few seconds later, he took a sip. The liquid gold tasted of smoke and fruit, and it warmed on its way down.

"Good idea?"

"Indeed."

Gregorio took a small drink. He closed his eyes and sighed. "I don't care what you say. This stuff can make anything better."

"Especially when someone else pays for it," Damien said wryly.

"Especially then," Gregorio agreed.

Following Gregorio's lead, Damien pushed away from the desk and relaxed against his chairback. He realized this was the first time in two weeks that he'd managed to release any tension without first spending an hour at the gym.

"So, you played with her outside of the Den."

"Mind your own business."

"More than once?"

"You know goddamn well I'm not going to answer that."

"Have you called her? Or are you waiting for Mistress Catrina to fall under your spell? Wait. No. Holy shit…" Gregorio uncrossed his legs and leaned forward. "Unless you subbed for her."

Over the top of the snifter, Damien regarded his second-in-command until the other man shrugged.

"Never mind that." Undeterred, Gregorio continued, "She subbed for you, which meant something since she's a Domme and sometimes shows up with multiple pets. And now you want her to become a sub for you. So, let me guess. You issued an ultimatum, you want her to do things on your terms. Ergo, you can't give in and call her."

"Ergo? No one really uses that word."

"Never mind." Gregorio nodded. "You have been waiting for her to come to you. Only she hasn't. And that means this is a unique situation for you." He took another drink then said, "How'd I do?"

"I'm relieved you'll be able to get a job as a psychic advisor when I give you your walking papers."

He expected Gregorio to be at least a little chastened.

Instead, the man all but crowed. "I did that well?"

"It's time for you to get back to work," Damien said.

Gregorio grinned and raised his empty glass in a silent toast before leaving the office and closing the door behind him.

Contemplatively, Damien ignored all the screens demanding his attention, and instead, stared out of the window.

With the frost on the trees, it looked fucking cold. And since the atmosphere was so dry, he doubted it would snow. Now, knowing Catrina wasn't planning to attend, he wished he'd stayed home. He had no desire to interact with anyone. And if he remained in his suite, he knew he'd brood.

Another sip of the brandy warmed his insides. In selecting the beverage, Gregorio had made an excellent choice.

Right now, it annoyed the crap out of Damien that Gregorio was right about so many things.

After Damien had finished the drink, he forced himself to go through Gregorio's plans and projected revenues for the upcoming month. Master Niles' former production company was requesting to expand their usage of the Den's facilities. And Gregorio had proposed buying an adjacent lot so the facilities could add onsite lodging to the five-year plan. Or at least a stable for pony play. Damien wasn't sure if Gregorio was serious about that one, or whether he'd snuck it in to see if Damien was paying attention.

An hour later, music blared, all but shaking the empty snifter still on his desk. Tonight's theme was retro-dance party. He couldn't wait to see what attendees came up with. Teased hair and leg-warmers? No doubt some would celebrate with high-protocol standards they no longer observed.

He hadn't anticipated, though, that Gregorio would hang a disco ball from the living room's vaulted ceiling. Or that Master Evan C's magenta scarf would look strangely appropriate for the party.

Damien realized he should have stayed in Denver.

He endured the evening, and it had been good to see Master Marcus with Julia on the end of a leash. She'd likely earned a beating for the way she'd wiggled her ass at Gregorio. At the very least, Master Marcus had compelled her to help serve the cupcakes, topped with neon pink or orange frosting.

* * * *

At five o'clock the next afternoon, he again checked the reservations list. Because snow hadn't fallen, at least ten more people had signed up. Catrina was not among them.

Two hours later, Damien had watched all the television he could tolerate. He'd finished his work and cleaned out his email inbox. Despite a shower, he was unable to settle in with a true-life crime story that had, until recently, engrossed him.

Restlessness churned at him. He tossed aside the book and strode to the closet. Telling himself he might as well be useful and meet with some of the potential new members — anything was better than dwelling on Catrina — he dressed in business attire and strolled downstairs.

After last night's craziness, bright colors, thundering noise, outrageous outfits and big hair, this event was subdued. Gregorio had put together an elegant mixer. Low-key jazz oozed from the sound system. No one had to shout over the band to be heard. Wait staff moved throughout the area with fruity, non-alcoholic beverages and canapés made from ingredients he would never touch but pretended to like.

He chatted with a few people in the living room, answered a number of questions about membership and various activities and gave one Dom some tips on dealing with a beautiful but very saucy sub.

Then, seeing Gregorio was occupied in the kitchen with the caterer, Damien excused himself. He went downstairs to check on the play area. The Den employed a number of House Monitors, men and women who knew the rules and enforced them to keep everyone safe. Regardless, Gregorio and Damien tried to make themselves as visible and available as possible.

He wandered down the hallway, looking in on all the private rooms, checking in on the participants. It had been a long time, years even, since he'd availed himself of the Den's facilities for a personal scene.

Until now, he hadn't missed it.

But at this moment, the idea of having a woman spread before him in beautifully bound supplication, helpless and writhing in expectation...

Damien inhaled sharply.

Maybe he should seek out one of the house subs to slake his sudden need.

In the open area, some couples sat at tables. A small group of Doms stood in a circle. One put his booted foot on his kneeling sub's shoulder. Looked uncomfortable for both of them.

Another's sub was seated cross-legged on the floor.

The final gentleman was alone.

After nodding toward the group, he crossed to the bar for a glass of sparkling water.

That's when he saw her.

Catrina was alone, seated at a high-topped table, swirling a straw in her drink.

He froze.

"May I get you anything, Master Damien?" a house sub enquired.

"No. Thank you, Mary."

She was a relatively new employee, having been hired to replace Brandy, whom Master Niles had stolen away and never returned. Even though Mary was tall, willowy, available and agreeable, the idea of taking care of his needs with anyone other than Catrina vanished. Truth was, even if she hadn't shown up, he wouldn't have beat another sub. No one but her would do for him.

She watched him over the rim of her glass, tracking his every move.

"May I join you?" he asked as he neared her table.

"Please."

Though he'd seen her on numerous occasions over the years, the more he knew her, the more there was to uncover. Tonight, no pretty man knelt by her side. In fact, there wasn't a leash in sight.

As usual at the Den, her makeup was startling. Her eyes appeared enormous, more luminous, thanks to false lashes. Her red-colored lips were full and pouty.

She'd left her hair loose, though a large clip held a chunk of it back from her face and showcased her stunning cheekbones.

By any standard, her black dress was demure, but fabulous. The square-cut neckline covered her breasts, but revealed her collarbone and an alluring glimpse of her cleavage. Previously he hadn't played with her nipples much, but now he itched to explore all of her.

"Nice event," she said as he sat.

"Quite," he agreed.

"I heard last night was a little different."

"I looked on the dessert table when I was upstairs. There isn't a single orange cupcake in sight."

"Orange?"

"They were a complement to the neon pink ones, I'm told."

"Sounds like fun. I love big hair and hoop earrings. I'll be here for the next eighties night." She moved her straw through the ice cubes in her glass. Her filmy shirtsleeve fell back, and he noticed her white wristband.

Gutted, he stared.

Any hint of ease between them vanished. Her smile, and her hand, froze.

To avoid confusion, when a guest checked in for the night, they were issued wristbands. Doms and Dommes wore red ones. Tonight, she wore white, which meant she was heterosexual and looking to scene.

He took hold of her hand. He kept his voice low and well-modulated as he said, "You're full of surprises."

"I decided to accept your challenge and try to submit," she said, meeting his gaze.

Damien rubbed his thumb pad against the flutter of her pulse.

"To you," she clarified.

"Of course it would be to me. This is my domain." No way would he stand by and watch her interact with anyone else.

She sighed. "You know you're arrogant, don't you?"

"Not usually, no." Confident, convinced of what he wanted, determined to get it...yes. But she brought out intense reactions in him that he wasn't sure he liked. "I'm not interested in a scene." He wanted so much more.

"I understand. That's why it took me so long to reach a decision."

"What convinced you?"

As if hypnotized, she stared at the small circles he made with his thumb.

He stopped rubbing and captured her chin and tipped her head back slightly. "No hiding."

"Maybe you can help me learn to be a better Domme. Maybe the experience will leave me unchanged. But there's only one way to know. And..."

He waited.

"I'm curious." She shrugged. "I liked what happened at your house. And the fact I enjoyed it scared me, shook me up. Worse, it made me question everything I've assumed over the last few years. Part of me wants to pretend it never happened. But the truth is, I'm also intrigued. It took me a long time to reconcile the different thoughts and feelings. How can I be a strong, independent woman, but then enjoy being in your arms after you spank me? I've spent years depending on only myself. The bigger question to me is...do I even want to consider a change? I've never met a man who was worthy of trust." She stared into the bottom of her glass. "And I like my life."

He waited, allowing the time to stretch in case she had anything else to say.

A full thirty seconds passed before she met his gaze. Her eyes were wide, honest. She placed her hands on the table, palms up. "It meant something when you said you'd always want your subs to come to you. I'll be honest. I thought that was a line. Or maybe a nice fantasy. The more I thought about it, the more I thought it sounded like friendship."

"I like that. Or maybe a partnership."

"Don't push it, mister."

He grinned. Now that she was near, the tension that had gripped him for two weeks seeped away.

"So I decided I'd talk to you about it and see what we could work out. I'll admit I'm intrigued." She wrinkled her nose. "Damn. And as much as I hate to admit it, I've already learnt a thing or two from you."

"I'm honored you'd say so. It's mutual. I've learnt not to assume what you're thinking. And I'm honing my patience skills."

"Oh, Damien..." She batted her eyelashes. "You've only just begun."

"I accept your challenge."

Catrina cocked her head to the right and more seriously added, "I want to know what else is out there."

"It will be an adventure for both of us." He realized he'd stopped rubbing her wrist, and he started again. "I want two weeks of your time. When can you arrange to be away from work?"

Her chest rose as she drank in a deep breath. No doubt this was becoming more real to her. So he continued his reassuring touch.

"I work from home, but I have to meet with clients periodically."

"We should be able to manage that," he said.

"My clients matter to me. I won't abandon them." She brought her chin up.

"I'd never ask you to. The things that matter to you matter to me. So let's figure out a schedule. Gregorio can set up an office for you. Just let him know what you need. I assume you have a notebook computer that you can bring? We have a satellite connection you can use for email."

"As long as I can get online, I'll be fine. I can pack all my files in a box."

"You can drive to Denver as needed. Or I can take you. I won't have you tied to my bedposts all the time."

"About that…"

He remembered her having a similar reaction at his house to his threat. "Scares you?"

"Yeah."

"You'll eventually ask me to."

His soon-to-be sub arched one of those sexy dark eyebrows. "I might agree if I tie you up a time or two."

"Not happening."

She tugged her hand away from him.

"Talk to me, Catrina, always. About everything. We can resolve anything as long as we keep the lines of communication open."

"That all makes sense. And it's great. In theory. But I'm not good at it. My first response, always, is to protect myself."

Damien was taken aback by how small and delicate she seemed. He'd always seen her as larger than life, a dominant, powerful force. Not that she wasn't still, but the hesitant side of her drew him. "Not all people are trustworthy," he said. "So it would be ridiculous to ask you to trust me." He covered her hand but didn't squeeze. Rather, he tried to convey his reassurance. "But I promise I will work to earn yours, every day, every moment."

"Let's start with one week," she said.

Damien shook his head. Certain things, he was willing to compromise. On others, he'd remain steadfast. The trick for him was in knowing which to choose when. "Two weeks is hardly enough time for you to explore what it means to live and breathe submission. A month would be better."

"That's not going to happen."

"I never thought it would." He'd only thrown it out there to make his dictate easier to swallow. He fingered her wristband. "You wanted to start tonight?"

"Yes. But I wasn't sure what your reaction to me would be since I hadn't called."

He would have waited forever.

"I didn't want to presume too much, and..." She paused. "I was a bit afraid of being rejected. I figured I could find someone to play with me." She shrugged fatalistically. "If not, I'd planned to trade it back in for a red one."

"Let me be clear about one thing." His gut was tight in an unfamiliar and unwelcome way. He looked at her hard. "As I've already informed you, my rules for you are slightly different than they are for others. If you're at the Den and you're subbing, it will be to me."

"That sounds a bit possessive."

"It is. Deal with it. So that we're clear, I will refund your membership fee."

She shivered.

"Problem?"

"Um." She exhaled. "I guess not. After two weeks, I'm going back to being a dominant, so arguing about the details is pointless."

"Well said. Now that I have you here, Catrina, I'd like to keep you."

"I didn't bring any toiletries or even a change of clothes."

"Jeff can pick them up. Just give me a list of what you need."

"You have a solution for everything," she said.

"Only the things I truly want."

To her credit, she kept her gaze on him, and she didn't look away, even though he noticed her shift uncomfortably. "As for clothes," he added. "You won't need many. I intend to keep you naked."

"Sounds cold."

"I'll turn up the heat. Anything else you want to discuss before I take you to a private room and make you scream?"

Chapter Five

Catrina's mouth dried.

Over the last couple of weeks, she'd played out a dozen scenarios in her head. She'd show up and he'd reject her. Or he'd frown and scold her. Best case, he'd fall at *her* feet. Still, she hadn't been prepared for this Damien, tender and simultaneously unyielding. It scared her when she thought of how easily she'd fallen under his spell.

His touch reassured, his voice soothed.

Sexual desire knitted her insides when he was close.

Earlier, she'd watched him come down the stairs. The first sight of him had stolen her breath.

As was customary, he wore all black. Tonight, though, his clothes had a more refined cut, and the fabric seemed richer, as befitted the elegance of the night. His trousers were tailored, his wing-tipped shoes polished. His sweater, she guessed, was cashmere. He looked every inch the owner and master of the place.

He'd swept his gaze over the gathered crowd, but he hadn't noticed her. He'd nodded toward several guests before continuing confidently down the hallway to check out the private rooms.

Everything about him oozed success and confidence.

She'd slipped over to the bar and secured a cola, knowing she needed to occupy her hands and her time until he saw her.

And she'd known the moment he had.

When he'd locked his gaze on her, she'd shaken, as if electricity had zapped down her spine. Courage had almost deserted her.

The way he'd moved toward her, with undeterred purpose, proved how much he wanted to dominate her.

And damn it, she'd spent two weeks denying the obvious. She wanted him to.

A sub had interrupted him for a moment, and she'd been momentarily afraid he would be needed elsewhere.

But he'd continued toward her.

Drawing on skills she'd learnt in an acting class, she'd pretended to be relaxed. She'd swirled her drink, thinking it was a metaphor for what was going on inside her.

And now that the rules were in place, he stood and offered his hand.

It was more than a polite gesture, she knew. It was his first demand. He was claiming her in one of the house's most public spots.

After only a moment's hesitation, she placed her palm against his. She accepted his strength as she slid from the high stool.

"Milady." He nodded, indicating she should precede him down the hallway.

That surprised her. He could have instructed her to follow him. He might have asked her to crawl. She should have realized that nothing about him was predictable. "Any particular room?" While each was furnished with a counter, sink and a few toys, none were identical.

Because a production company rented space here, she knew there was a storage area that contained an amazing array of furniture and contraptions.

Almost every fantasy could be fulfilled with enough notice.

Some rooms had no doors so that participants could be watched by anyone who wandered past. Others could be sealed off, except for a small window. All scenes were looked-in on at some point by either Gregorio, Damien or a designated House Monitor.

"Last one on the right is vacant."

She'd never been down that far, and she wondered what he had in store for her.

Gregorio intercepted them on the way. "Enjoying the evening?" he asked, his arms folded across his imposing chest.

She detected a hint of a tattoo on one biceps.

The man glanced between Damien and Catrina, obviously taking in their body language.

"It's okay to ask her if she's willing," Damien said dryly.

Gregorio nodded. His pirate-like earring glinted in the dim light, and his bald head made him seem all the more imposing.

Like the trusted employee he was, Gregorio asked, "You're not under any undue pressure, Milady?"

"I'm here of my own free will."

"And you know the Den's safe word?"

It gave her comfort that Gregorio was looking out for her, even where his boss was concerned. "Halt," she said.

"I'll be looking in on you." He cocked his head in his boss's direction.

"You're not invited to join us," Damien said. "She's mine."

Gregorio grinned. The expression was quick, as if he was satisfied in a very personal way. "I never thought otherwise, Boss."

"Please prepare an office for Catrina on the second floor."

Gregorio dropped his arms. "Private?"

"Adjacent to mine."

"By when?"

"Monday morning. I have plans for Catrina tomorrow."

"I take it our meeting is canceled?"

"Not at all."

Gregorio frowned.

Obviously she wasn't the only one confounded by Damien.

"Consider it done, Boss. Milady, please, if I can be of service, let me know."

"Enough," Damien said, the word a growled warning.

Without saying anything further, Gregorio stepped aside.

Feeling Damien's fingers possessively resting against the small of her back, Catrina continued down the hallway. As they reached the end, he reached over her head to push open the door.

She missed a step as she crossed the threshold.

Nothing could have prepared her for what she saw.

A gigantic spool-looking contraption dominated the space. Though she didn't know what it was called, she knew two ways it could be used. And in either case, she'd be completely helpless to him.

He placed his fingers lightly at her spine again and urged her forward.

"I'm not a masochist," Catrina warned him. She turned to face him once she was in the room, several feet away from the torture device.

"Not yet," he said.

Her knees went weak. "Damien…"

"I was teasing you," he said softly. "I won't do it again."

She appreciated that.

He turned away to close the door.

It made a tiny *snick* as it sealed, and her heart pounded loudly in her ears.

"It has no lock," he said as if he'd read her fear.

She knew that. For the protection of subs, few doors at the Den had locks. But she'd momentarily forgotten that.

Damn. The mindfuck that happened when she submitted obliterated her rational thought.

"Milady, I'll never ask you to do something that will cause you bodily harm."

She glanced over her shoulder.

"I'll release you anytime. You have a safe word."

Which meant he intended, at some point, to affix her to the blessed thing.

Catrina was learning that her thought process was more dangerous than anything he could do to her.

"We'll go as slow as you need."

She noticed he hadn't offered a different room. No. Instead, he was enforcing his will in subtle, inexorable ways. And she was drawn into his spell.

He took hold of her shoulders.

At the table, he'd run his thumb pad over her wrist, back and forth, as well as in small circles, helping keep her calm. Until tonight, she'd never fully comprehended the power of a Dom's touch.

Sure, she rubbed her boys' heads, ruffled their hair, ran a finger down their cheekbones, stroked their cocks to the point of distraction and even imprisoned their faces so she could make eye contact. This, though, was different. His intention was to form a bond that drew her closer to him, deeper under his spell.

"What would you like me to call you?" he asked.

She hadn't thought about it. Her mother referred to her as 'my Cat'. Some of her closest friends had nicknamed her Trina. Clients and friends used her given name. "Catrina is fine."

"Do you object to me calling you Milady?"

She tilted her chin and met his gaze. "As long as you're not saying it in way that mocks me."

"If you think I would ever do anything like that, Catrina, you don't know me."

His voice was tight. A pulse ticked in his temple. She'd never seen that happen before. The Damien she knew was calm, never ruffled. But she'd unintentionally pissed him off. And she was glad. It told her he respected her.

"I know how much this took for you. I will never underestimate it, and I will always appreciate it. Your being here, what you're offering me, is a gift. I will cherish it. And you," he replied, his voice soft and all the more forceful because of it.

She glanced away, but she felt his gaze on her. Relenting, she looked back at him. "Thank you," she said simply.

Even if the words were as difficult as the concept was foreign, respect went two ways. "How should I address you?"

"Damien is fine. I prefer Sir."

She sank her teeth into her lower lip as she nodded.

"Master is a term of great respect. I do not demand it. If you feel I deserve it, if you get to that point, then I'd be honored. But I do not expect it."

Catrina nodded. Common courtesy, she understood, as did he. But acknowledging someone as her master? Verbally admitting capitulation by calling him Sir? Not likely.

"Please strip." He spread his legs and waited.

Since she'd been naked for him one other time, this should be easy enough.

She removed the clip and the weight of her hair spilled down her back. Then she grabbed the hem of her dress and pulled it upwards, over her head. He held out a hand for both items.

"Black shelf bra. Nice choice."

"Thank you."

He regarded her.

"Thank you, Damien."

"You make some classy choices, Milady," he said, taking in her stacked heels, garter belt, stockings and a wisp of fabric that counted as panties. "Completely naked."

She shook off her shoes, leaving them tipped over on the floor. Catrina took her time unfastening the clasps then rolling down the stockings.

When he growled impatiently, she hurriedly removed the rest.

"I might keep you in nun's clothing," he said. "It might be the only way I survive this. You have curves in all the right places, Milady."

Nervousness ebbed away.

He gathered up everything and placed it on the counter.

"Would you like to know what we're going to do?" he asked when he returned. "Or would you rather it be a surprise?"

Every word he uttered had power. "Surprise me," she replied. Knowing what was coming might build fear.

He nodded. "Over the spindle."

"I was afraid that was coming."

"Are you flexible enough to be on your back?"

"I think so."

He helped her into place.

The equipment was big enough that the stretch was more comfortable than she'd expected.

"Make sure everything's okay before I attach you."

Her hair fell down behind her. And if she didn't try to lift her head, her neck didn't hurt. That had its own disadvantages. It made it harder to see what he was doing.

Her feet didn't quite reach the floor, but her calves rested against the wood, supporting her lower body.

"Arms back," he said, crouching near her.

"Maybe I should have said I couldn't do this position."

"You would have wondered what you were missing."

"It's a little unnerving to think how well you know me already."

"Milady, your expression gives away everything."

He secured her to ties she hadn't before noticed. Keeping a close eye on her, he tightened the bonds. "Your movement is nicely restricted?"

She tested their strength. "Yes, Damien."

After placing a gentle kiss on her forehead, he stood. The gentleness of it undid her.

"For my security, I'm going to fasten your ankles."

Her legs were parted, which meant her pussy was exposed to him.

Now that she was helpless, her pulse raced. Damien was fully dressed in street wear, not even club attire.

She wished she could see him better, but being facedown would have been worse.

Since her vision was restricted, her hearing seemed more attuned than usual. His footfall echoed, and she guessed he was walking toward the counter. For a condom? "Are you going to fuck me?" she asked.

"Do you want me to?"

"If it's part of the scene."

He said nothing.

The sound of a squeak indicated he'd opened a cupboard door. His expensive shoes ricocheted off the room's tile floor as he returned to her.

"I like to look at you, my pretty little submissive."

She opened her mouth to protest but then closed it again. Right now, she was assuming that role.

"That's right," he said. "*My* pretty little sub."

Though she knew what he expected her to say, she couldn't respond.

"You know I can do anything I want to you."

Catrina closed her eyes. For a few seconds, she considered using the house safe word, but the panic receded. He could only do what she wanted. That was the magic of the power exchange. Being on this end was deliriously thrilling.

"I've been thinking about your nipples, wondering how much tension puts you on that edge between pleasure and unendurable pain. Have you ever had them clamped?"

"No."

"Then we'll start with some tweezers."

"I thought I told you I didn't want to know what you would be doing to me," she said wryly.

"Your wish is my command."

A few moments later, he was standing above her, legs parted. She was looking up at him, scant inches from his crotch. Suddenly she wished he were naked.

He took hold of her right breast.

She closed her eyes.

He toyed with her, plumping it. When she moaned, he increased the pressure. When she whimpered a little, he decreased it. She drew a grateful breath, but he repeated the squeeze. Before she could yelp, he'd backed off again. His touch was light as he skimmed his fingers toward her nipple.

For a moment, he did nothing.

Then he touched her ever so gently. "Good?"

"It is."

"And this?" He increased the intensity of the pinch.

"Fine," she responded.

He tugged.

She arched toward him as much as her bonds would allow.

"You're okay with quite a bit of pressure, it seems."

"I like that." As much as she hated to admit it, he was right about so many things, including the fact it had been a long time since a man had been focused solely on pleasing her.

"It turns you on?"

"It does," she admitted.

"Makes your pussy wet?"

She wondered if he could smell her. "Yes," she whispered. "Yes, Damien."

"And both nipples together?" He pinched and pulled and rolled them between his thumbs and forefingers.

"God, yes!"

"Would you like to come already?"

"Yes, yes, yes." She tried to lift her hips, silently begging him to bring her off.

"I think it will be more intense if you wait."

"I don't want to wait," she protested. She tried to meet his gaze, but he was infuriatingly focused elsewhere.

"You'll be okay," he said, his tone reassuring in a way that did nothing to lessen her dismay.

He leaned over and affixed the clamps.

"Damn!"

He adjusted the pressure.

"The tighter I make them, the hotter you seem to get."

"Damn you," she said. "I want an orgasm."

"Oh, Milady, you'll get more than one."

Her clit felt swollen, and her whole body tingled.

"If I'd had any idea how you'd react to me, I'd have tied you up and dragged you in here weeks ago."

"You've got me now," she said, barely able to form the words. "Make it worth my while."

"Gutsy words, Milady." He chuckled.

Damien continued to master her as he chose, not how she wanted. That realization magnified the experience so much more.

He crossed to the far side of the room, leaving her helpless, aching, wanting.

Before she was ready, she felt leather strands hit her belly. She gasped.

"Red is definitely your color."

He beat her, criss-crossing her tummy, her breasts, flicking at the rubber tips that gripped her nipples. He didn't vary the impact much, and that silently let her know what to expect.

Damien took a step back then made bigger motions, now hitting her pussy. She yelped each time one of the broad strands caught her most tender flesh. She felt scalded from the inside out.

"I can't... I can't..." She thrashed her head.

He continued until her teeth chattered.

Nothing seemed to exist beyond the thunder of her heart, the ragged sounds of her breath and the reality of his leather caress.

If he were her sub, she'd grab hold of his head and drag him between her legs, compelling him to eat her until she came with a scream.

But movement was impossible, and she could no longer think.

"That's it. Let go."

Of what?

He seemed to be everywhere, and when he squeezed one of her breasts while flicking at her cunt, she understood.

Instead of straining against the bonds, desperate to get her needs met, she relaxed instead. She allowed the smooth wood to take all her weight.

"Excellent."

She closed her eyes. When each blow landed, she breathed into it.

Instead of wanting the scene to be over, she could continue forever.

Sound receded. Nothing existed but the moment, the sensation of him slapping her with the flogger and its delicious stinging pain.

Then, suddenly, she became aware of...nothing.

Before she could react, Damien licked her pussy.

Sensation flooded her. She screamed as she came.

But he didn't stop.

He reached up to flick her nipples where the clamps seized them.

He licked and sucked, fucking her with his tongue, conquering her.

"Damn. Damn, damn, damn!" She came again and again.

He lifted his head and gave her cunt a few sharp slaps with his hand, then laved away the hurt.

Impossibly, she orgasmed again.

She'd rarely had multiple climaxes, preferring instead, to savor one and recover from it. And the only time she'd had more than one, she'd been masturbating with one of the world's most powerful vibrators.

"I want you for myself," he said.

She wasn't sure she could endure anything else.

"You're perfect, Catrina."

He loosened her legs then cautioned, "Move slow." He rubbed her skin, bringing some circulation back.

"Mmm." She figured this counted as aftercare. And she liked it enough to make sure she spent a little extra time with her subs in future. The high after a scene like that was stunning, and the figurative distance to the ground was vast. A slow descent was better than a fast one.

He loosened the nipple clamps by slow measures so the blood didn't rush back in with debilitating speed. He caressed her breasts then sucked the tips, easing her pain.

"Thank you," she said.

"Take your time," he instructed as he unfastened her wrists. "I'll help you to sit up."

She winced as she moved. Even in that short length of time, her shoulders had stiffened.

He stood at the side of the spindle. She expected him to offer a hand, but instead he supported her head and back as she wriggled forward.

"Stay there," he said when she was sitting. He made little circles on her shoulders to help loosen the stiffness.

Even without her saying a word, he seemed to know what she needed.

"Your body is a lovely shade of red."

"It feels well used."

"Not quite," he said. He helped her to stand and held her so close she felt his erection, inhaled the scent of his crisp masculinity. His arms were both strong and gentle. A tiny part of her brain betrayed her, whispering that it was okay to lean on him and drink the comfort he offered.

She pulled away from him before she could give in.

"Time for part two of your lesson."

"I hope it's as good as this one. I hate to be disappointed."

"I have a gag the perfect size for that mouth," he said easily. And he meant it. He went to the far side of the room and returned with a penis-type gag.

"I...ah...was joking." No way could he really mean to put that in her. Bravado deserted her. "I thought you wanted your sub to come to you and discuss things and that you'd agree on a punishment beforehand. You said that. Right?"

"You're being mouthy and you did it on purpose."

"I was teasing."

"So what would you do with a sub who was disrespectful?"

He kept some distance between them, but because he was dressed in business attire and she was wearing nothing but the stripes from his flogger, she was at a disadvantage.

As tall as she was, Catrina wasn't accustomed to that position.

And why had she taken a sensual moment between them and tainted it with her sass? He was giving her a moment to explain. "I'd ask him what had compelled the behavior," she said, remembering their discussion at his home. Her gaze flicked to the penis gag.

"So, why did you respond that way?"

"Nerves," she replied. "I liked the spindle, and I didn't think I would. I liked the beating, and I didn't think I would. I had a number of orgasms, and I'm still restless." She lifted her hands then let them fall again. "I apologize."

"You drove an intentional wedge between us."

"Yes," she admitted softly.

"Hoping to piss me off."

"I seem to do that a lot."

"And if you do it again?"

She licked her upper lip.

Damn it. This was part of the reason she didn't do relationships. It was simpler to play with her boys then send them home. "Why do you have to complicate things?"

He smoothed her hair back from her face. "Is that what I'm doing?"

"If I'd wanted a relationship, Damien, I'd have gone looking for one."

"You knew what to expect when you showed up here. Yet you came of your own free will."

"The gag would have been easier than this conversation."

"It might have been." He dropped his hand. "But remaining silent would prevent you from destroying whatever intimacy we were building."

His question stood. Now that they were both aware of her behavior, how should he handle it in the future? It occurred to her that she'd done the same thing before, in her relationship with Todd. She'd been so desperate to not be hurt again, she'd kept him at a distance with her sharp comments.

Damien had been serious when he'd told her he intended to eradicate her barriers.

"I want you to be who you are." He fisted a hand in her hair and pulled back her head so that she couldn't look away.

This Dom amongst Doms offered no quarter, as he imprisoned her gaze with his searing blue eyes.

"No, correct that. I want you to be your authentic self. I want to know the real you, the woman you really are, not sub, not Domme, but the whole, complete person you are when you're not scared."

Those words terrified her.

"Your quick wit is part of your personality, and I want you to share that. But question your own motivation, Milady. Are you being funny? Or are you trying to drive me away?"

The column of her throat was exposed to him. He still held the gag, but that didn't stop him from placing the pad of his thumb in the hollow of her neck.

She felt humbled that he cared enough to continue to move toward her emotionally rather than pull away as Todd had done.

"I'll know *you*, Catrina. Nothing less."

Trapped, unable to avoid his scrutiny, she nodded.

Slowly he released his grip on her hair, but he held her shoulders until she regained her balance.

"I'm waiting for my answer."

"A spanking," she said. "If I say something disrespectful, I think you should spank me."

"Nice try."

"I'm not sure I understand."

"There isn't a single misbehavior that will earn you a spanking, Milady."

"I thought we got to agree on something together."

"Together," he affirmed. "So spanking is off the table. Once you're over my lap with your bare bottom upturned, I can only think of bringing you off. Trying to spank you would torture me."

The way he said it, so rich, so husky, she believed he meant that. "The gag it is, then."

"Hopefully we won't need it."

She glanced at it. The part that would go in her mouth seemed enormous. "It certainly seems like a disincentive," she said.

He traced her upper lip with a finger. "Turn *to* me," he encouraged her.

"I'll try." She offered nothing else. No false promises.

"You may put on your dress and shoes as we go through the public area. I'd prefer you naked and gagged, however."

"No gag."

"I think it would be hot."

"Is that all you think about?"

"Since the first time I had my hand on your bare skin," he confessed.

She trembled. The way he looked, coupled with his tone, made her certain he meant it.

He picked up her dress and held it while she wriggled into it. "You make an excellent ladies' maid," she said.

"When the woman in question is you, it's an honor."

While she put on her shoes, he tidied the room and gathered her undergarments.

"You could put those in your pocket," she said when he opened the door. Silk, satin and lace dangled from his grip.

"I could."

But he didn't.

On the main level, they garnered a couple of curious glances. Long-time members knew she was a Domme, so seeing her with Damien must have been a shock.

When she'd checked in and asked for a white wristband, the house sub at the door had called Gregorio over. He'd ensured she knew the meaning of what she was doing.

"This is better than any fireworks on the Fourth of July," Gregorio had said before personally helping her into the wristband.

She'd gone downstairs and stood at the bar. A Dom she often conversed with had joined her and started to chat. When he'd noticed her wristband, his attitude had changed. Since he was alone for the evening, he'd invited her to join him for a scene.

The idea hadn't appealed.

She would sub, but only for one man.

She'd made her excuses then sat at a table where she'd be less approachable.

"We'll continue up to my quarters," Damien said.

Like many people, she'd wondered about the off-limits parts of the Den. There were rest rooms upstairs that were available to guests but a door sealed off a big section of the third floor.

Gregorio was leaning against the balustrade, and he pushed away when he saw them approach.

"The production company could use you as a model," Gregorio said to her. "Your height shows the spindle off to its fullest effect."

"How long did you watch?" Damien asked, voice tight.

"The whole time."

"And by that you mean?"

"Thirty seconds. No longer. Just enough to be sure everything was okay." He held up his hands. "Promise."

She'd be the first to admit she didn't know Damien all that well, but his behavior seemed unusual.

"We'll see you tomorrow."

Gregorio nodded.

"Milady? Shall we?"

She started up the stairs, and he was right behind her.

Within a few seconds, she was inside, sealed off in silence. She'd expected to see a big bed. Or a living room. Instead, they'd stepped into an enormous open space. Off to her right was a wall of windows, complete with a set of French doors that presumably led to a deck.

An enormous desk loomed in front of her. "Yours?"

"It is."

Like she expected, there was no mess. The surface was bare, except for an empty brandy snifter.

He rounded to the far side of the desk and deposited her undergarments on a chair. He put the blasted gag on top. "I hadn't realized you'd brought it," she said.

"It was more than an idle threat, so I figured we'd keep it close."

Did he forget nothing?

He opened a drawer and pulled out a remote control. He aimed it at the wall behind her. She turned, surprised to see dozens of images, each showing a different place on the property. She saw people getting out of cars, checking in at the front desk, milling in front of the hearth, heading down the stairs. "Command central?" she asked. "Unless you have serious voyeuristic tendencies?"

"I'd rather participate than watch." He pushed a button, and the pictures vanished.

To her left, there were two cubicles, separated by a thick sheet of glass that was etched with a mountain scape, an eagle soaring above a peak. "Your choice. They were both prepared for you."

She chose her words with care. "You expect me to work here?"

"There's someplace you'd rather be?"

"Anywhere." When he'd instructed Gregorio to ready an office for her, this hadn't been what she was expecting. She'd thought there'd be walls between them, doors...distance. "I'll never get anything done with you so close."

"I'll shackle your foot to the desk."

Catrina wrapped her arms around herself. "I'm not sure whether or not you're joking."

"I'm not."

"That's what I'm afraid of." She'd played with him in private, been to his secluded house, yet nothing had felt more intimate than this.

"Would you like to see the rest of the place?"

His domain.

He gave her the code that would open the opaque glass door. "We can leave it open if it's more comfortable for you," he said.

"Whatever you prefer."

His grin made her pulse stammer.

He closed the door.

While not overly large, the space was wonderful. Glossy hardwood floors were covered with numerous throw rugs. A couple of tables were placed strategically, and a chair sat next to a leather couch, and both faced the television atop the gas-burning fireplace.

He had a small kitchenette, complete with coffee pot, small refrigerator, sink and microwave oven. "I feel like I'm at a luxury hotel."

"That was my designer's intent. I don't always want to go downstairs for my coffee. And I prefer my own deck for my first cup, especially if anyone has stayed over."

"You're not a morning person?" It astounded her how little she knew him, and how much she was about to learn.

"I prefer some quiet time before I engage with others. Let me finish showing you around."

The luxury continued. His bedroom had a walk-in closet. He had a built-in dresser, a few shelves and a rod. Several pairs of black slacks hung next to dress shirts and a couple of suit coats. He had a sexy pea jacket, a leather bomber and an entire selection of ties. All his shoes were in individual cubbies. Even the dirty laundry in the wicker basket was arranged by color and fabric weight. He had a ridiculous number of belts, and the idea of one of them hitting her bare butt made her back out of the closet.

A king-sized bed faced a window, and two nightstands only had artistic, elk-antler lamps on their surface. His bathroom was tiled, with double sinks, a soaker tub and a shower big enough for two. "I want you to be comfortable here. Ask for anything you need." He met her gaze. "Except privacy."

"Do you spend all your time coming up with words to terrify me?"

"Of course not."

He backed her up until a wall stopped her.

"No?" she asked.

"I also think about the dozens of ways I'd like to fuck you." He took a step back. "There's a box of condoms and a bottle of lube in a basket in the linen closet. Fetch them."

He left her behind in the bathroom.

Because everything was so perfectly organized, she found the items exactly where he'd said they were.

She joined him in the living area again.

"Put them on the mantel."

He'd turned on the fireplace and dimmed the overhead lighting, bathing the room in a soft glow. He was seated in the chair, an ankle propped on his knee. He never took his gaze from her. She wasn't sure anyone had ever paid this much attention to her, ever. She tried to give the scenes with her subs all her concentration, but rarely for this long.

There were no personal effects in his space, no pictures, no knick-knacks. There hadn't been any in his office, either. Clearly he'd left everything the way the designer had arranged it. She had an urge to clutter things up, shake him up as much as he unsettled her.

"It's really quiet in here," she said, voice hardly over a whisper. She'd expected to hear some sound from the music, the dozens of guests, even the comings-and-goings of vehicles.

"I like my privacy. And I want you to have the freedom to scream all you want."

"I've told you, Damien, that's not likely." She placed the items where he instructed then turned to face him again.

"You do like to challenge me."

"I think it's time someone did."

"Be careful where you step, Milady."

"Thanks for the warning."

"Come here, Catrina." He stood and extended his hand, a gesture that looked like an invitation, but that she knew was a command.

She came to a stop in front of him. He took her shoulders and drew her even closer, closer than was comfortable for her.

He released one of her shoulders and moved his hand to her face where he tipped back her chin. "I promised you lesson two."

"Lesson two?"

"Concentrating, fully, on pleasing your Dom. We'll start with you undressing, we'll continue with you undressing me."

Chapter Six

Catrina had watched his scene-setting demonstration that night with Susan. Now she realized he'd only offered a glimpse at the weapons in his arsenal. His tone seduced her. The way he touched her sent her pulse skittering. Even the silence added to the atmosphere, seeming to amplify what little noise there was.

It was the spell he wove with his words, though that stirred her imagination in a way that could have been an art form.

Though they hadn't been sexual, she was already dazed.

"Proceed," he said, releasing her.

Her legs felt wobbly as she took a step back.

As she had earlier, she removed her dress. He nodded toward the couch, and she draped the material over the back.

"We'll keep the wrist band. I like what it symbolizes. Oh, and leave the heels on for now."

"That male thing again?" she asked.

"Turns out I'm suddenly an ass man. Much as I loved seeing you displayed on the spindle, I'd like to put you over it the other way, just for my edification." He sat. "Start with my shoes."

It was one thing for a man to kiss her feet, it was another to be at his. She considered crouching, but that would give him a glimpse of her pussy. So that left kneeling as her only option. "Too bad you're not wearing boots. I could straddle your leg to get them off."

"I'll wear a pair tomorrow."

Bastard probably would, too.

She knelt and untied his laces before removing his shoes and socks.

He stood. "I'm at your mercy, Milady."

Since she was on her knees, it made sense to remove his belt. She tugged the leather free and rolled it up before placing it on top of one of his shoes. She contemplated dropping his trousers, but she needed a minute to prepare herself before having her mouth mere inches from his cock.

Ignoring the way his lips twitched in a half-smile, she stood. She removed his sweater and tossed it near her dress, pretending not to notice his wince. Yes, it was definitely time to shake up Damien Lowell.

She unfastened his trousers, and let them fall down. "Boxers, Damien?"

"I like my balls loose," he said. "But wool can chafe. I can wear something else if you prefer?"

"No. I like the way I can reach my hand in the front of boxers."

"Do it."

He already had an erection, and she closed her hand around him. "Silky," she said as she moved her hand back and forth. "And I love how thick it is." She might have said the same words to a sub, but there was a difference when the man intended to dominate her with it.

A few strokes later, he clamped his hand around her wrist. "That's enough."

She was accustomed to deciding when enough was enough for a man's dick. And most times, it was a couple of seconds before he spilled. But she gritted her teeth and instead took off his boxers.

He stepped out of his clothing.

"Remain as you are."

Knowing she'd never get away with leaving his pants on the floor, she hung them from the couch. The boxers, though, she wadded and tossed beneath the couch.

"Play with your nipples," he instructed.

"They're already sensitive from your clamps."

"All the better."

She rolled them and squeezed them and tugged on them, aware of his perusal, of the pre-cum leaking from his cockhead.

He took hold of a handful of her hair and she whimpered a little. "I want you to look up at me."

Compelled, she had no choice.

"Now play with your pussy. But don't come."

She fingered herself.

"Slick already?"

"Very," she said. In the absence of any other instruction, she continued to slide her fingers, then she dipped inside.

"I can smell you," he said.

"Yes." She'd had so many orgasms earlier that she thought it would take her forever to get turned on. But she already felt as if she were close to a climax. Her whimpers became moans.

All embarrassment disappeared as need built.

"That's a girl," he said. "Play with that gorgeous pussy."

As the edge neared, she moved faster and faster, jerking her hips, trying to get better angles, more pressure.

She stopped caring how tight he held onto her, and she closed her eyes. So close...

"That's enough."

When she didn't immediately respond, he snapped, "Catrina, stop!"

She blinked and froze.

"Lick your fingers."

Frustrated, she made an exaggerated show of sticking out her tongue and curling it around her fingers. All the while, she kept her gaze fastened on his face.

"Sexy," he said. "I like the added sound effects. Been watching some of Master Niles' videos?"

She dropped her hands to her sides.

"I know this is an adjustment for you, that you're accustomed to being the one who decides what to do and when to do it, so I'll be more patient than I normally would." He pulled her head back a fraction of an inch. "I'm mentioning it, however, so you'll know I'm aware of your behavior. If it happens again, we'll need to discuss it." He loosened his grip and continued in a gentle tone. "There's something magic that happens when you get out of your own head, like you did when we played downstairs. It's only two weeks. Yield, Milady."

She didn't respond. It was one thing to strategically prevent her sub's orgasm. It felt different when she was the one experiencing pins-and-needles sensations along her inner thighs.

Catrina pressed her legs together, hoping to alleviate some of the stress.

"That won't help."

As always, he was right. In fact, her efforts seemed to make it worse.

"I'll always insure you're taken care of. Your satisfaction is mine." He let go of her hair. "You can't believe I want to deny you."

At this moment, with frustration crashing into her, it seemed that way.

"Get the lube, Catrina, and a condom. You can use your mouth to put it on me."

She often put condoms on her boys. In fact, she loved doing it. She could tease and prolong, never letting him know what to expect. Keeping her sub guessing was one of her favorite things to do.

Again, this was different.

Damien wasn't asking her to do anything she didn't normally do, but her frame of mind was different. Interesting how the same act could be submissive or dominant, depending on her attitude.

She crossed to the fireplace and was very much aware of him watching her.

"You have one fine ass, Milady."

As she pivoted to face him, she tossed her hair over her shoulder.

"Can't wait to fuck it."

"I'm ready to get on with it," she said. The sound of her shoes seemed to ricochet in the silence, which was a good thing. At least it covered the sound of her thundering heart.

She couldn't take her gaze off his cock. How in the hell was she supposed to use her mouth to roll a condom down that?

"Quit thinking so much." He spread his legs.

She'd thought he'd looked imposing while fully dressed in own-the-world business attire. Now, he was devastating. His thighs and calves were defined with muscle. His stomach was taut. His biceps were cut. It seemed his clothing only made him appear civilized.

He helped steady her while she knelt.

She placed the bottle of lube on the floor then fumbled the condom package before managing to get it open. Then she checked to be sure she had it on the tip of his cock correctly. "No hands?" she asked.

"Mouth only."

After drawing a steadying breath, she used her mouth and her tongue to unroll the confounding thing.

"Think about me," he instructed, cradling her head in his palms.

She looked up, drew a breath then went to work, making it as erotic as possible for him.

"That's it."

When she touched her tongue to the underside of his cock, he jerked toward her. So she added a little more pressure before pulling away and repeating the action.

With her hands curled on her thighs, she worked the latex lower and lower while returning to caress his most sensitive spot.

"I should have you give me a blowjob every day."

Not that she'd mind.

As she got the condom almost in place, she started to gag. Her eyes watered, and he was so big he filled her mouth, hitting the back of her throat. Using her hands would help tremendously.

"Almost there." A few seconds later, he said, "Good."

She pulled back, and tears spilled out of her eyes, ravishing her make-up, she was certain. He didn't seem to mind. He used his grip on her upper arms to pull her upright.

His cock pressed into her stomach, and he kissed the top of her head. "You're gorgeous, Catrina. *And you're mine.*"

Those tender touches would be her undoing. His powerful gentleness made her want to lean into him.

"I'm going to fuck you from behind. Make no mistake about who is your master, Milady."

Catrina was so far gone, she didn't take exception to what he said.

"Brace yourself on the back of the couch."

Finally. She got into position. Her pussy moistened from her excitement. The way he looked at her, touched her, responded to her sucking created a dynamic she'd never had with anyone else.

"Your cunt is so plump." He toyed with her until she all but danced and whimpered, desperate for his possession.

She felt his cockhead at her entrance, and she lifted up onto her toes to allow him greater access.

"Perfect."

"Take me, Damien."

"Patience, Milady." He entered her slowly, surely, resisting her when she wriggled her hips backwards. No matter what, this man refused to allow her to hurry him.

He took hold of her hips and held her while he drove into her.

She cried out when he was up to his balls in her pussy.

"Scream for me, Milady."

It was almost impossible not to with the way he fucked her, pulling out, thrusting in, filling her completely.

Her breaths became ragged.

"Hold on a little longer."

She gripped a cushion, seeking purchase while he claimed her. "Damien."

"Wait for it."

Catrina gulped in breaths.

All of a sudden, he stopped.

He pulled out, and she turned her head. The curtain of her hair made it difficult to see exactly what he was doing, but she heard him squirt lube onto his hand.

"I'm not sure I'm ready for that."

"When I fuck your ass, Catrina, I'll make sure you are."

She let her head fall forward again. So far, he'd given her nothing she couldn't handle.

He inserted a slick finger in her anus. She swayed, allowing him access.

"Now a second."

She gasped. The second finger gave her more than double the sensation.

He put his dick back in her heated pussy. Her body shook as he simultaneously pounded her ass and cunt.

"Damn, damn."

Reality became a blur. An impending orgasm churned in her. She wasn't sure how long she could last, no matter what he wanted.

Then she screamed when he reached around her and pinched her clit.

The climax crashed over her.

She bucked and cried, and he was unyielding, riding her, forcing her to accept his penetration until he, too, came. She shuddered and held the cushions with a death-grip.

The relief from the orgasm was short-lived. The physical release left behind a wake of relaxation, but the emotional residue clobbered her.

"Was the wait worth it?"

He gathered her hair and held it back.

She'd never experienced anything so profound. He'd devastated her, yet she ached to turn to him for comfort. How the hell was she supposed to sort through this whole thing? She'd wanted to experience the things she put her subs through, but nothing could have prepared her for the stunning reality.

"Hmm?" he asked.

Her first reaction was to fire off a smart-ass comment, but she was aware he'd brought the penis gag upstairs. She'd promised to try to be more honest, but the cost to her defenses was steep. It took all her courage to admit the truth. "It was fabulous, Damien."

He withdrew his cock and eased out his fingers before helping her up and turning her to face him. "I'll draw you a bath."

"Shouldn't I be doing that for you?"

"And you can peel my grapes while you're at it," he said.

She hadn't thought of that, that he might expect her to cook and clean for him. Wasn't that part of what a sub was supposed to do? What the hell did she really know beyond a Friday or Saturday night hook-up?

"I'm self-sufficient, Milady. I don't need a housekeeper or personal chef. And I know my way around the grocery store. I even know how to operate all household appliances."

"It's kind of creepy how you do that. Read my mind."

"Wish I could say that I had that kind of talent, but your face is expressive. You gasped when I made the grape comment."

She followed him into the bedroom, and he invited her to select one of his T-shirts while he went into the bathroom.

"I thought you wanted to keep me naked."

"Most of the time," he called back over the sound of running water. "But I also don't want you to catch a chill."

Catrina opened one of the drawers and selected a T-shirt from the bottom of the pile. She went with a soft, well-worn one.

"I have some without holes in the hem."

"This is comfortable."

"Good enough for me."

"I need something for my hair."

"I'll be right with you."

She sank into the bath water while he left the room. He came back holding the clip triumphantly.

"Thanks for remembering it."

"It was tangled with your stockings," he admitted.

She bent her head while he piled her hair atop her head. "You're hired," she told him.

"I could play with your hair all day."

Damien showered while she soaked.

Sharing the bathroom like this was unique for her, and she lay back and enjoyed the warmth and the fact he was so near.

"Next time, I'll shower before you drain the water heater," he said a few minutes later.

She opened her eyes as she sat up to see he'd wrapped a white towel around his hips. His raven-dark hair curled at his nape. Beads of water clung to his torso. Was there anything sexier? "I should apologize," she said, "but this feels too wonderful for me to be sorry about your cold shower. I'm afraid my muscles would have been sore without the bath."

"Are you playing the poor-me card?"

She grinned. "Would it work?"

"Like a charm. You can have all the baths you want."

He took a towel from the linen closet and wrapped her in it when she climbed out of the tub.

Although they hadn't spent a lot of time together, she was already expecting him to hold her and give her a kiss, which he did after releasing the clip from her hair. The dichotomy he represented fascinated her. Strong and tough yet soothing and responsive.

In the bedroom, she reached for his T-shirt.

"I'll keep you warm," he said, plucking the material from her fingers and tossing it on the end of the bed.

"So I'm sleeping with you?"

"You've behaved well enough for me not to cuff you to the headboard. And definitely well enough not to make me tie you to the footboard."

"You wouldn't."

"Try me."

Again, the combination of rigidity that contrasted with his protectiveness. It kept her off-balance. "You mean it."

"Every word, Milady. Never forget I'm a Dom."

As if she could.

* * * *

"How was your lesson?"

Catrina wiggled her upper body to better prop her bare shoulders against the headboard and regarded Damien over the rim of her coffee cup. He'd awakened her by wafting the steam near her nose. Smart man.

He'd helped her sit up, then offered her the brew.

She'd taken a sip and sighed in bliss. He'd made the coffee the way she liked, which meant it was strong enough to dissolve a spoon.

He moved to the far side of the bedroom and sat on the window sill.

She wasn't sure how long he'd been up. Long enough to dress in a pair of jeans and—God help her—nothing else.

Even if he hadn't reminded her of the sex they'd had last night, the first sight of him would have brought it back. "I thought you weren't a morning person," she said, stalling.

"I was thinking of reinforcing it if you hadn't learned it well."

Unbelievably, his words aroused her.

"I woke up craving your pussy," he told her. "Yesterday I fucked you from behind. This morning I want to see your face as you cry out my name."

"That's not—"

"You screamed last night."

"I didn't." She sipped and noticed that her shaking hand made the coffee slosh. "Did I?"

"Yeah. Sweetest music I'd ever heard. I'll give you five minutes."

She frowned in question.

"Finish your coffee. Do whatever you need to in the bathroom. Put a condom on the nightstand and be on your back on the mattress, knees over the edge, legs spread as wide as you can get them."

Without another word, he left the room.

Knowing he meant what he said, she took a big gulp, wincing as the heat scalded her mouth.

She dashed into the en suite and was touched when she saw he'd laid out a brand new toothbrush for her. She found a washcloth in the linen closet and scrubbed off her remaining make up. The eyelashes would last a few more days.

The box of condoms was still on the hearth, but he wasn't in the living room. For not being a morning person, he went to work early, even on a Sunday.

Just under the allotted time, she lay back, naked.

He kept her waiting, and she was sure he did it on purpose to let her mind turn somersaults.

She took a few steadying breaths, then attuned her hearing to listen for him.

Despite hearing nothing, she stayed where she was.

"What a good girl."

She froze. How the hell had he entered without her hearing, and how long had he been there? "Do you have a camera in here?"

"Our bedroom is a sanctuary, Catrina. No cameras. When we're in our suite, I share you with no one."

"So that means you were standing there, watching me," she said.

"Always. I told you there'd be no privacy."

She gripped the sheets, unsure if he meant that as a threat or a promise.

"Part your labia, Milady. Use both hands."

Trembling, she took hold of each pussy lip and pulled it back.

"Keep your legs right where they are while I spank your pussy."

"But..." She closed her eyes, remembering this was supposed to be a lesson.

"Unless you need a spreader bar?"

"I'll stay in position." She jerked when he abraded her clit.

Nothing but the sounds of their combined breathing disturbed the atmosphere. Even though she'd been moist as she'd prepared for him, she was now dry.

It was difficult, but she kept her hands in place.

He pulled back the skin to expose her clit. She tightened her buttocks. He didn't reprimand her, and he didn't do anything else for a long time, just kept her there, exposed in the most terrifying way.

Thinking about him.

Her heart raced, but she remained where she was.

He touched her clit with a fingertip that was warm and moist. She should have known his touch would be kind — should have — but hadn't.

He gave her pussy a couple of gentle swats, enough to help her relax. Then a few more to arouse her, then a few more that made her cry out from the sudden shock, then several open-handed, hard slaps that hurt so fucking bad that it turned her on.

"God. Damn." She started to pull her hands away so she could protect her cunt, but she kept them in place.

"Tell me what you want."

"Your cock. Put it in me, Damien." She writhed, silently urging him to hurry.

"So pretty, all swollen and red."

"And wet."

"It is, isn't it?"

She felt his tongue on her, soothing and exciting. "Please, please."

"Hands above your head."

His sheathed cock was at her entrance, but then he took hold of his penis and moved it across her pussy, teasing her with it.

"I'm going to go crazy," she warned him.

"You're thinking about yourself."

He was right. She was at such a fevered pitch, she was no longer considering him. "Yes, Damien," she said. Her resolve to concentrate on his pleasure lasted for all of three seconds before she lifted her hips to envelop him as he thrust forward. "Yes," she said around a gasp.

"Look at me."

She opened her eyes.

His face was only inches from hers. His blue eyes had never seemed so compelling, and she couldn't look away. He placed her wrists one on top of the other and encircled them with one of his hands.

"You can come after I do."

"Not sure I can wait that long."

"It'll be two days before I let you climax again if you don't follow my instructions."

"You're dastardly."

He grinned, and it made him seem all the more intimidating. "I could screw you for the rest of the morning, Milady."

"Please don't." She was already fighting back an orgasm with every breathing technique she'd ever learnt. The way he held her and fucked her blazing cunt had her teetering on the precipice.

Damien used his free hand to play with her nipples, driving her mad.

She felt desperate to close her eyes, certain it could help break the bond.

"Look at me," he reminded her.

Instead of fighting, she kept her gaze fastened on him, drinking in strength from the set of his jaw. She met his surges and whimpered with each one.

"Beautiful," he said. "So beautiful in your surrender." He released her wrists and pushed a thumb against her clit.

"Damien! Damien," she pleaded.

"Legs around my waist."

The change in positions gave her moment of respite, but ultimately it put him deeper inside her.

"*Now.*" He impaled her then jerked inside her a few times, his ejaculate pulsing from his body.

Using her calves as leverage, she ground out her own orgasm, sobbing as she splintered from the inside out.

"You're an apt student," he said when she turned her face to look at him.

"The teacher provides plenty of motivation, though it might be fun to stay after class."

He pulled out and helped her get back on the bed properly. "Rest for a minute," he said, and joined her, tucking her head beneath his chin.

Across her body, his arm felt heavy, and she didn't mind.

"I've decided I'll go to Denver with you today."

She rolled over so she could look at him. "What happened to sending Jeff?"

"He has the day off, and I didn't know that until I checked the schedule this morning. And before you suggest it, you're not going alone. You'll spend too much time inside your head and freak out."

"I don't *freak out*," she protested.

"No? Then what's happening right now?"

His radar was keen. "Maybe a little. You can be a bit overwhelming."

"We need to take some of the tension off. Enjoy the day."

She narrowed her eyes at him.

"We'll leave in half an hour, grab some breakfast on the way."

It sounded suspiciously mundane.

Nothing with him ever was, though.

She was overdressed, or underdressed, depending how she looked at it, for the rustic mountain lodge where they ate. He hadn't given her back her undergarments, so she was aware that her nipples were hard, and she was sure everyone knew she had on no panties.

No one, though, gave her a second glance. Skiers and snowboarders were talking about the weather, conditions on the slopes and discussing the runs they were going to get in. Locals looked at newspapers and the national news broadcast.

He ordered steak and eggs, with a side of salsa. No carbs.

She went straight for the specialty, *migas*. She'd never had them before, but they sounded delicious, three scrambled eggs with jalapenos, green chillies, tomatoes, gobs of cheese and tortilla strips. "I need my energy to keep up with you," she said while biting into the accompanying banana walnut muffin.

He finished a few minutes ahead of her. "Impressive," he said.

"Now I need a coffee," she said, when she forked the last bite of potatoes from her plate.

"We may need to hire a cook if you're going to consume a couple of thousand calories at every meal."

"Or stop exercising so much."

"Eat up."

She grinned and raised her juice glass in his direction.

They grabbed a to-go latte from a local coffee shop before hitting the road.

"You're a great chauffeur," she said. His sedan was all luxury, with heated leather seats and individual temperature controls for the driver and passenger sides.

Her side was ten degrees warmer than his. Then again, he had on jeans, boots and a cable-knit sweater.

She sipped the vanilla-flavored latte while he told her about his business ventures and gave her the history on how the Den had come about. His wife had been an avid skier who had a large family. She'd envisioned it as a place for family retreats, holidays, reunions.

"You were married?" she asked, putting the drink in the cup holder. How had she never heard that juicy piece of gossip?

"Didn't last long."

"I had no idea. What happened?"

"Nothing," he said. "It was unremarkable. Margot and I married. Things didn't work out. We went our separate ways. End of story. No great devastation that left me emotionally crippled."

"Quit holding out."

"We started dating when I was in grad school, then we got married a year or so later." His grip on the steering wheel was light yet competent as he negotiated a hairpin curve while climbing Berthoud Pass. "I got a job at a private equity firm. Getting married seemed like the next logical step. But I was at least as fascinated by money as I was with my wife, and I worked a lot of hours, including weekends."

Catrina turned in her seat to face him. "What happened to the marriage?"

"Things fell apart when she realized she didn't want to be my sub anymore."

"Wait. What? Sub? You left out whole chunks of the story."

"Frustrating, isn't it?"

She collapsed against the seatback. "I get it."

After a few seconds, he relented. "A bunch of us frat brothers flew to a friend's bachelor party in Vegas. We went to a BDSM club. It was my first visit, and I was hooked. I'd known I had dominant urges, but until that night, I didn't have a term for it. My girlfriends had just thought I was an overbearing jerk. They were probably right."

"You bossed them around?"

"And ordered them to suck my dick while I pulled on their tits." He had the good grace to wince. "I'm not proud of it."

"Now you make women beg for the privilege."

"I hope my technique has improved over the years."

"Yes." She remembered the way her body had felt last night and the ultimate, crashing satisfaction he'd given her. "I can say it has."

"It didn't come easily. I joined a BDSM club out by the old airport. At a demo one evening, the instructor suggested Doms switch roles. I wish I could say it was my idea, but one of my subs told me I should give it a try."

"Sounds as if you had a rough go of it, ego-wise."

"When you're told your sexual tactics need improvement? But she was right. Getting a swipe from a cane taught me that I should be a bit more careful with how I wielded one."

She shuddered. Canes intimidated her. It was part of the reason she didn't use one unless her boy requested it. "Was the sub Margot?"

"No." He glanced her direction. "I met Margot at a concert, and by then I was upfront about my lifestyle and what it entailed. The idea of doing something scandalous thrilled her, at least initially. After we were married, she didn't find it as exciting. She was bored and restless because of the amount of time she was spending alone. And being my slut princess every night when I got home close to midnight lost its appeal. She found someone less demanding and more available."

"I wonder how that's working out."

"She misses it."

"How do you know that?"

"Ran into her recently at a dinner party."

"And the two of you immediately had a discussion about BDSM?"

"She brought it up."

Jealousy nipped at Catrina. She shoved the emotion away. He could play with whomever he wanted, even his ex-wife.

"I don't scene with married women, unless their husbands are there. And her fourth husband, Larry, has no intention of letting her anywhere near me."

"Can you blame him?"

"He's a retired pro wrestler. Could still pile-drive me straight into the ground."

The image was laughable. "I'd stay away, too. Seriously, no lasting repercussions from the divorce? You haven't remarried."

"No need." He slid her a sidelong glance. "I have my businesses and my fill of beautiful women."

The unwelcome envy slithered back in. "Seems a little superficial, maybe even lonely."

"We all make our choices, Catrina."

She crossed her bare legs. The man had a way of saying things that made her see her own life, as if he were holding up a mirror in front of her.

"There are times when I'd prefer the company of others. That's part of why I have the Den along with a circle of close friends. I've no desire to marry again."

"I thought you performed Julia and Master Marcus' wedding."

"It was an honor to do so."

Before she could ask another question, he held up a hand to stop her and added, "Don't get me wrong. I understand why some may choose to do so, and I respect all of those reasons, especially the legal and financial ones. But I have no need to do it again."

"How did you end up with the Den?"

"Gregorio had thought of the business possibilities, so I bought out Margot's interest. It's turned out to be a solid investment."

"You don't miss having someone to share it with?"

"As I said, there are trade-offs."

"Are you afraid of falling in love again?"

"That seems like a romantic question, coming from you."

"Ironic, isn't it?" she asked.

"In answer to your question, I was never in love to begin with."

She faced him, her mouth open. "Never?"

"As I said, getting married seemed like the next logical step. I cared for her deeply. I was committed to her. Ultimately that wasn't enough for either of us. Anything beyond affection never entered the equation."

"You don't believe in it?" she pushed.

"I haven't thought about it much, but no. I suppose not. You?"

"Been there, done that, and I'm a quick study. Once was enough."

When they neared Denver, she directed him to her bungalow.

"Nice area," he said.

"Yeah. I love Wash Park. Great for people-watching. Lots of dog walkers, coffee shops, boutiques and lunch places."

"You hungry again?"

"No. Haven't burned any calories."

He came around and opened her door. She pulled her lapels tight against the chill.

Inside, he said, "Lots of potential."

"Lots of time," she added. "And money." She could have hung their coats on hooks. But she chose to fling them over the back of the couch. "I bought it as an investment a few years ago. I fix it up a little every year."

"Solid thinking," he said. "I approve. Mind showing me around?"

The kitchen was the first room she'd improved. She had granite countertops, top-of-the-line appliances and had installed a window over the sink.

"Nice backyard."

"Much better in summer when I have potted plants blooming."

He followed her into the living room. The hardwood floors were dull and splintered. "On the to-do list," she said. As was, eventually, building shelves to hold her knickknacks, photos, books, magazines and DVDs. As it was, every surface was covered, with items stacked on top of one another.

Next up was her office.

"Nice job in here, too."

"This was the easiest room. Less trim work here, and the floors were in fairly good shape since the previous owners had used it as a guest room. While I'm here, I might as well grab my files and computer."

She didn't excuse the clutter. She was a creative thinker who left notes and ideas in every corner. She hadn't met a piece of paper she didn't want to write on.

He held a box steady while she filled it. "What do you do, exactly?"

"I'm a financial advisor." She tossed her favorite pen on top of the folders. "For women."

"The former fiancé who wiped out your bank account?"

"You were listening."

"To every word you say."

He said it so honestly that she had no choice but to believe him. "After I picked up the pieces, I used it as motivation." She met his gaze. "To advise others how to rebuild or carry on after the loss of the primary earner. Eighty to ninety percent of women, at some point, will be solely responsible for their finances."

"I like your style. You took something painful for you and used it for good."

"Wasn't just for me," she admitted. "My mom, too." She smiled at the memory. "She was my case study. If you can get your mother to listen, you're doing okay. She's always believed in me, but to do what I said with the small amount of funds that she did have... She made a plan, set some objectives, read a whole bunch of prospectuses, did some research on her own. She's still a few years away from being able to retire, but I got her to double the amount of money she thought she might need."

"Impressive."

"Most times, women are not prepared for the shock of their loss, and then you throw in retirement funds, or lack thereof, debt ratios, bills..." She shrugged. "I get most of my business through referrals, and I have a group that meets monthly where women set goals and share their frustrations, help one another with strategies."

"Different approach than I've seen men use."

"Turns out the sexes are different, Mr Lowell."

"You don't say."

She put her computer in a backpack, grabbed her phone charger then led the way back to the living room. Part of her couldn't believe she was going to do this.

"I want to see your bedroom."

"I'm just going to throw a few things in a bag," she said when he placed the box near the front door. "You're welcome to watch television or have a drink while you wait. I have beer in the fridge."

Not surprisingly, he followed her. "Where do you keep your lingerie?"

She sighed and pointed to the dresser. "Third and fourth drawers."

"Grab your suitcase."

Since there was no point in arguing, she did as he said.

He selected a few items and tossed them on her bed. "Shoes?"

"In my closet."

He added a pair of stupid-high sandals to the growing pile. Surrendering to the inevitable, she gathered her toiletries from the master bathroom while he started going through her street-safe clothes.

"You can wear this," he told her when she returned.

She was relieved to see he'd selected a pair of jeans and a long-sleeved T-shirt.

"No bra."

"I'd figured that much."

"When you play with your subs, do you go to their place, or do they come here?"

"They come here."

"Where do you play?"

Catrina knew where this was going, and she didn't like it. "The other bedroom."

"Show me."

"That's…" She hesitated.

"Private. Your domain?"

"Yes."

"Then that's where I'll master you, Catrina."

"Is that really necessary? We can go back to the Den."

"There, as well." He nodded toward the open door. "After you."

Chapter Seven

This gorgeous woman appealed to him on so, so many levels. Her eyes were as green as they were revealing. And her face, devoid of make-up, hid nothing. All her concerns were clear in her expression, including the fact her eyebrows were drawn together, and he sensed an impending argument. Having no intention of indulging that, he acted, picking her up and tossing her over his shoulder.

"What the hell are you thinking?" she yelled, kicking futilely. "Put me down!" She pummeled his back.

He swatted her upturned derriere.

"Ow! Damn you, Damien."

Undeterred, he strode to the end of the hallway.

He carried her past the beautiful black, oriental screen that hid a kneeling bench. He put her down next to it. "Take off your shoes, please."

She glared up at him.

"Use the safe word or do as you're told." When she did neither, he said, "What's the punishment for defiance?"

"Talking about it," she said.

He fought to hide his grin. "The punishment is having to talk to me?"

"Yeah." She folded her arms across her chest protectively.

"Go on." He sobered.

"I don't know what's wrong," she admitted. "This makes it... I don't know. More real."

"It hasn't seemed so until now?"

"No. It's been more like... Playing at a club. I could be detached in a way."

"I hear what you're saying." He allowed her to keep a small distance between them. "And that's why it's crucial we do this."

"If we do it here, it's part of my life." She looked away.

"Safe word. Otherwise I'll push." He gave her a few seconds to think it through then repeated, "Please remove your shoes."

She scowled. A full ten seconds ticked by before she complied.

"Thank you."

"Thank you?"

"I know this isn't easy, and I appreciate you yielding to me."

"Don't get too cocky."

"I assure you, Milady, you'll never let that happen." He knew trust didn't come easily, if at all, to her. All day, he was sure, she heard stories of failed relationships and hurt. No doubt that reaffirmed her resolve to protect herself. "Now the dress."

She removed it and dropped it on the floor.

"I could have hung that up for you."

"I know."

"Trying to bring a little disorder to my life, Catrina?"

"Me?" She blinked innocently.

"I'm onto you." He walked around her. "Please put your hands behind your head and spread your legs."

"You going to inspect me, Damien?"

"I am."

She wouldn't be allowed to goad him into losing his temper. But he would give her a taste of what it was to submit, totally.

"This is under duress."

"Duly noted." He gave her time, but she followed his direction rather than using her safe word. "You really are a treasure, Milady."

"Don't patronize me."

"I was sincere," he said, walking around her. "I don't say things I don't mean. I don't need to."

She continued to look ahead.

"You're tempted," he said.

"To?"

"Look at the floor."

"No."

"As a show of respect."

"No."

"As a submissive act."

"No," she said, the word all-but a breathless whisper.

"As an acknowledgment that I'm your Dom."

"No."

But as he circled her, she did what he asked. "Lovely." He stopped in front of her and trailed his fingers down her chest, between her ribs, over the stomach that trembled from his touch, past her pubic hair then between her folds.

She jerked.

"Slide yourself back and forth. *Do it.*"

"Yes, Damien." She moved her pelvis against his hand.

"That's it. Pretend you're fucking it."

"I—"

"Stop thinking."

She gyrated her hips, and he felt her become wetter.

Usually he talked to his subs, encouraging, engaging, soothing. But he forced himself to remain silent while she worked through her emotions.

Her back loosened, and she no longer held herself as rigid.

That's it. He slid a finger into her moist cunt. She moaned. He knew the instant she'd managed to let go of her thoughts and surrender to him. She humbled him.

He decided to let her have the orgasm she was working toward. "Take it," he told her.

She curled her toes then slammed her heels against the floor as she came.

He wrapped an arm around her back to support her as her knees weakened. He moved his hand and gathered her close, holding her.

"I didn't know I could come this many times," she told him.

"We're consuming some of those calories so I can take you to lunch later."

"A man after my heart," she said.

"I hope so. When you're ready, please kneel on the bench."

She looked at it, then back at him.

He stepped away from her and went to the closet where he found her Domme stash. "Anything in particular you want to explore?"

"Ah, no. All of those things were designed for a man's tough hide."

"I think you'll find yours is much tougher than you might have imagined."

"I was afraid you would say that."

He pulled out a flogger then selected a cane. When he turned back to her, she was kneeling as he'd instructed. "Ever felt a cane?"

She paled.

"It can be vicious," he said. "But it doesn't have to be. You no doubt have subs who want varying degrees of intensity."

"And?" Her voice wavered.

"A good Dom can deliver that with almost any implement."

"I'm skeptical."

"Timing and arousal and location all factor in. Certain body parts are more sensitive than others. And of course, the way I wield it matters more than anything."

"Still not buying it." Her gaze was riveted on the thin, reedy piece of rattan.

"Enough talk from me. I'll let you decide for yourself."

She stood. "I'm good with skipping this lesson."

"Would you like to be tied?"

"No…" She paused.

He thought, for a moment, she might call him Sir. Then the moment passed and she resumed the position he'd requested. "Thank you. You please me, Milady."

"Can we get this over with?"

"My pleasure." And he intended to make sure it was hers, too. He brushed aside her hair and kissed the back of her neck.

She rolled her shoulders.

"I'm going to flog your back."

"Fine."

Damien sighed. At no point had he thought this would be easy. He hadn't expected it to be so difficult, however. She, though, was worth any cost. He moved all of her hair across her left shoulder, and softly said, "I'm marking you as mine, Catrina."

She gripped the bench until her knuckles whitened.

He trailed the broad, thin strands over her exposed skin. He flicked it back and forth. "What would you do to relax an uptight sub, Milady?"

"I'd keep talking to him," she said. "And I'd start easy."

"Would you now? Even though a man has a thicker hide, in your words."

"Absolutely."

While he'd been distracting her, he'd been slowly using the flogger on her, letting it fall with a gentle sway. "How would you know if your technique was working?"

"His breathing would change. He may perspire a bit…" She trailed off.

"Then what?"

"His muscles wouldn't be quite as tight. So I'd be able to actually see that he wasn't as nervous as he had been."

"Right."

"Eventually he'd stop running his mouth."

Damien grinned. He noticed that she'd loosened her grip. Since her skin was starting to appear dewy, he made his hits more random, across her back, her buttocks, even her feet. He took a step back so he could get more leverage on his swing to give the blows more impact.

Her head went a bit slack.

"You're doing well, Milady." She was *his*. Surrendered. But he wanted to reinforce it in a more serious way.

He switched out the flogger for a cane. With the tip, he tapped the soles of her feet.

She curled her toes and her body tensed.

"Shh," he said, skimming her neck with kisses.

"Oh…"

"That's it." He moved back again and laid a few light stripes across her buttocks.

"Uhm. Ah…"

"Too much, Milady?"

She hadn't clenched her ass cheeks, and that was a good sign. "Milady?" he asked again.

"I'm okay, Damien. I…"

"You?" he prompted. He continued his strokes, not adding a lot of variety.

"Like. Like it."

His cock hardened. This woman, beautiful in her submission, thrilled him. He wanted to hold her, cherish her. "Keep trusting me, Milady."

Her hair fell forward to shroud her face as she braced herself.

With the lightest of motions, he struck the bottoms of her feet.

She cried out.

"That's right. Scream. Cry all you want. But savor it."

"I…"

He hit her again, harder.

She jerked her feet away.

"Back into position." He moved so that he could trail his fingers up the insides of her thighs. "You'll be glad we did this," he promised her.

"No," she insisted.

He played with her pussy, finding her damp. "Oh, yes," he said against her ear. "Do you want to come for me?"

She didn't respond, but she shifted against his hand, silently imploring him.

He manipulated her until she began to whimper.

"Damien, Damien, Damien." She didn't pause, making his name sound like a chant.

He pulled back and used the cane three times, much harder, on each foot, making her convulse and scream before he tossed aside the rattan and dropped to his knees behind her, fingering her pussy, her ass, pounding her as he reached around her to drag her upper body back so that he could support her completely.

Sobbing, she came, her pussy clenching.

After removing his hand, he soothed her, kissed her. And when she started to shake, he picked her up from the bench and carried her into the living room. He shoved aside a blanket and several magazines before sitting on the couch and pulling her toward him. Holding her tight, he cradled the back of her head, one of her cheeks pressed to his chest. He splayed the other on her upper back. This, this was where she should be.

He stroked her hair and uttered soothing words.

"That was…"

Curious, he waited.

"Amazing."

Her answer, along with the way she'd reacted to his physical domination, turned him on. This woman, independent and strong, yet so trusting in his arms, was starting to get to him.

She twisted slightly to look up at him. "If you'd have asked me if I was willing to try that, I would have refused. I had no idea the cane could be so stimulating or so nasty. And hitting my feet…?"

"What did you think?"

"I hated the idea. I honestly considered using my safe word. But because it scared the shit out of me, I wanted to prove I could do it."

"You have nothing to prove to anyone, to me, to you. No one. Do you understand me?"

"Yeah." She wiped a knuckle beneath her eye to mop up a stray tear. "But you don't know me, clearly."

Her words made his gut twist. "You need to hear me, Catrina. And I mean it."

She met his eyes, and he saw her take in the set of his jaw. "As much as you trust me, I need to be able to trust you. Have you ever had a sub use his safe word?"

"A couple of times."

"Did you think less of him?"

She worried her lower lip. "I wouldn't have done anything that would have hurt him."

"You never, ever know where someone is mentally, emotionally, physically or what scars they bear from previous experiences. I will never judge you. But the biggest part of this relationship is about honesty. You'll have to give me everything you have. *Everything*. And that includes exposing your fears."

"You don't ask for much," she said wryly. "You want honesty? Well, this is as real as it gets. No one will get that deep inside me ever again. My submission is yours for two weeks. Nothing more. That's the agreement." She put her hands on his chest, creating a physical barrier. "Nothing more," she reiterated.

Sierra Cartwright

"Know this, Milady"—he captured her wrists—"I will spend the entire time trying."

"I wish you luck."

He'd seen it, though, the way she'd glanced down and to the left as she pushed herself off his lap. His Domme wasn't as sure of herself as she wanted him to think. He warned himself to be doubly vigilant where she was concerned.

She went into the bedroom to dress.

When she returned, she'd secured her hair with a ribbon. The black jeans clung to her hips, and she'd tucked them into a pair of stiletto boots. Her legs looked to be miles long, and the near-knee height of the leather was giving him a hard-on. No doubt she'd been deliberate in her selection. "Obviously your feet don't hurt?"

"Not at all."

The long-sleeved T-shirt he'd picked out showed the feminine swell of her breasts. "No bra?"

"I always do what you say."

"Uh-huh."

"Would you like to see?"

"I would."

She blinked.

"Show me."

"Seriously?"

"Show me."

With a sigh, she grabbed the hem and lifted her shirt, showing her gorgeous tits and still-swollen nipples.

"I suspected you'd followed orders."

"So you were being a pervert, Damien?"

"Yeah. Because I can."

She grinned and their earlier tension dissipated. Her phone rang.

"Anyone important?"

"It's my mom."

"You're allowed to talk to her."

She twisted her lips.

"Unless you're gagged." He carried the box and her luggage to the car and waited with the engine running.

A few minutes later, she locked the front door and knotted her jacket's belt as she walked. Not that that was a good word. This woman oozed class and seduction, and she more resembled a model on a runway.

She slid into the passenger seat and turned to look at him.

"Problem?"

"We're having lunch with my mom and her new boyfriend."

"We are?" He watched her until she fastened the safety belt, then he eased away from the curb.

"Yeah. Sorry. I couldn't get out of it."

"I'm looking forward to it. Where are we going?"

"There's a brew pub at Denver west. Steaks aren't bad."

"You're hungry again?"

"You would be, too, if you'd been beaten."

"Good point." The farther west they drove on I-70, the quieter she became. He slid her a sidelong glance. "Everything okay?"

"Yeah. Fine."

"It's okay to talk about it."

"My mom's getting married."

"Congratulations?"

"I've never met him."

"Is that a prerequisite?"

"You don't get it," she said, staring straight ahead.

Rather than argue, he suggested, "Enlighten me?"

She was silent for so long that he thought she might not answer. "They've known each other less than six weeks. In fact, until recently, I didn't know she was dating. I don't know anything about him. Hell, she can't know anything about him. And they're already shacking up."

"Meaning, they're living together?"

"You say that like it's okay." She scowled.

"She is an adult, I presume. Of sound mind?"

"I thought so, until this."

Wondering why it suddenly felt as if he were navigating a minefield, he asked, "What's your concern?"

"I wish she'd slow down, make sure she's making wise decisions."

"You're assuming she's not."

"Whose side are you on, anyway?"

"Yours." He took her hand. "Always."

Catrina reclined her seat a little. "She made a disastrous decision with my dad."

"That was at least twenty-five years ago, unless I'm mistaken." He waited until she nodded to confirm his guess. "Other than that, does she have a bad track record?"

"No. She's dated a little, and she's had some long-term relationships. But that doesn't mean I like this." She drummed her fingers on the dashboard. "Nor does it mean that I think you have a point."

"Of course not." He exited the highway at Colfax. At a red light waiting to turn left, he flicked his thumb across her fluttering pulse.

"It's just sudden. You think I'm crazy?"

"No. I think you care. I think you want her to be as cautious as you'd be."

"Thanks for that."

The light turned green and he accelerated. "Does she know I'm with you?"

"Yes. You're a business associate whom I've known for a few years. We see each other from time to time. Nothing serious."

"That works." He nodded. "Close to the truth."

"Better than telling her you made me strip and kneel before caning me."

"Good call." They exchanged grins, and he saw her vulnerability beneath her tough-girl exterior. He wanted to see that more and more.

Her mother and boyfriend were already seated at a table with large mugs of beer on the table when Catrina and Damien arrived.

"When did you start drinking beer?" Catrina asked after introductions were performed.

"I've developed quite a taste for it," Evelyn said.

Catrina kissed her mother on the cheek but limply shook Milton's hand. Damien pinched her ass before they sat down. "Behave," he warned against her ear.

Catrina shuddered, but she didn't protest.

Evelyn, bursting with enthusiasm, started talking about their upcoming wedding plans. The woman surprised him in some ways. Both she and her daughter were tall and slender, but Evelyn was as outgoing and vivacious as Catrina was reserved. It made him double his determination to break through her shell, prove the world wasn't an unsafe place.

The server dropped off menus and silverware then nodded when Catrina ordered red wine. Damien took Milton's advice and asked for the house amber ale.

"Traitor," Catrina whispered.

"Brat," he responded with a smile. Then he looked at Evelyn. "When's the big day?"

"Next month," Evelyn said.

"Next *month?*" Catrina repeated.

"The chapel isn't available any earlier than that."

"Any earlier? You just met," Catrina responded. "What's the rush?"

"Young lady, I assure you we don't have to get married," Milton said with a grin.

"Miltey!" Evelyn scolded, but she ruined it by laughing, and the two clinked their beer glasses together.

"So will it be a large wedding?" Damien asked.

"Small," Milton said. "A few hundred people, our closest friends and family."

Catrina straightened her spine.

"He's kidding, my Cat. We're only inviting those closest to us."

"How did you meet, anyway?" Catrina asked.

"Miltey and I met online."

"You use the Internet, Mom?"

"What, you expected us to say bingo?" Milton deadpanned.

Damien already liked the man.

"He sent me a flirty little heart icon."

"Because you captured mine the minute I set eyes on you."

The pair made eye contact as if no one else were there. Catrina played with her rolled-up silverware, looking a bit pale.

Recognizing how difficult this was for her, he placed his hand on her knee. She went still for a moment then he felt her fingers swirl across his knuckles.

The server dropped off drinks and took food orders.

Damien kept the conversation light, telling them about some of his business ventures.

"So, that's how you and my Cat met?"

"We share similar interests," he replied as he squeezed Catrina's thigh.

"Well, Cat, you're welcome to bring a guest to the wedding." Evelyn looked at Damien before taking another drink of beer.

Damien and Milton wrangled for the check. Damien promised to let Milton pay the next time they all went out.

"That was nice of you," Catrina said as they walked to the car. "Unnecessary, but nice. They could have split the bill four ways."

"It's okay to let people do things for you. For example, this." He opened her car door, waited for her to get settled then sealed her inside.

"I'm not used to it," she admitted.

"Our two weeks together are about learning."

She didn't respond, and he headed west on the highway.

They were almost to the Evergreen exit before she spoke again. "Do they still do that part in a wedding ceremony where the minister asks if anyone objects when a couple gets married?"

"I'm afraid not."

"What harm is there in them waiting until they know each other better?"

"How long is that?" he asked.

She tugged on her safety belt. "I don't know."

"A year? Five years?"

"Longer than a few weeks."

"If it's right, it's right. Time doesn't make a lot of difference when it comes to matters of the heart. You can know in two weeks if you want to be with someone. And you can still be uncertain after five years."

"I hadn't figured you for a romantic."

"More of a realist," he countered.

"I'm not sure how you consider that realistic."

"Doesn't it somewhat depend on how they spent their time together? What if they've been talking? Sharing their secrets."

"Look, if you mention the fact my mother may be having sex, I will wash your mouth out."

"They are living together, it makes sense that they're doing the—"

"No. Just…no."

He chuckled.

"I need to talk to her about protecting her financial interests. Maybe I'll suggest that she put together a prenuptial agreement."

"Or consider the possibility she knows what she's doing."

She exhaled. "You don't ask much."

"Look, Milady. She raised you. I think she did okay."

"I'm not sure what to say about that. I think it's supposed to be a compliment."

"Do you think you'd be able to change your mother's mind?"

"About Miltey?"

"I'm warning you, Catrina. Give him a chance."

"Or you'll give me a spanking?"

"Or I'll withhold a week's worth of orgasms."

She turned up the heat on her side of car. "He seems nice enough. Which is why I'm suspicious."

"You'd be suspicious no matter what."

"You might be right about that. And no, I probably won't be able to change my mother's mind."

"So be a good little sub and focus on making me happy."

Catrina laughed.

He raised an eyebrow and looked across at her. "You could pretend to go along."

"Yeah. But I'm not going to."

Then she stunned him by reaching across the cab to touch his forearm.

"Thank you," she said. "For going with me. I appreciate it. Having you there helped."

"Anything for you, Milady." He was surprised how much he meant it. "I enjoyed myself. I liked Milton's sense of humor, and your mom's a firecracker."

"She volunteers for a hundred different things. And she is still a substitute teacher."

Catrina dropped her hand. For safety, that was probably a good thing. Catrina's touch was magic, but it was a hell of a distraction.

They stopped at a grocery store on the way into town. He picked up a basket and headed for the produce section as he asked, "How are your feet? You okay to walk through the whole store?"

"They're a little tender, but nothing bad."

"I was hoping every step would remind you of the way you were caned."

"It is now," she said, glaring at him.

"Bananas?" he asked, holding up a bunch.

At the checkout counter, she added three bars of chocolate to their purchase. "I may need to keep up my energy," she said.

He tossed another one on top.

By the time they arrived home, the sun had already set and the sky resembled inky velvet.

"This is a whole different place when there's no party here. Peaceful."

The grounds were brilliantly lit, but the house was mostly dark. A light was on in Gregorio's quarters across the way. Other than that, it seemed they were on a hundred acres of deserted land.

He parked his vehicle in the garage then grabbed the groceries and her luggage.

"May I help with some of that?"

"Open that door. We'll take the back stairs."

"You can come and go as you please without anyone knowing you're here," she said when they reached the top. "Like a superhero."

He juggled groceries and set down her bag to unlock the door to their suite. "After you."

"Wait, give me a minute. I'm enjoying the image of you in a cape and a sculptured suit. I'm thinking tight pants, too. Really tight."

"I'll give you something else to enjoy."

"Will you, Master Damien?" she asked, her voice oozing with sensuality.

He put down the shopping bags, dropped her luggage then took hold of her shoulders and backed her against the wall. "Open your mouth."

She did.

He traced her lips with his thumb, and when her eyes fluttered shut, he took hold of her wrists and pinned them above her head. "That's my girl."

"Damien…"

He kissed her, tasting the first hint of resistance then the sweetness of her response as she opened her mouth wider. Their tongues mated and he insinuated his leg between her thighs. Damien plundered her depths, teasing, retreating then advancing again, deeper. She relaxed into him and rubbed against his thigh.

Yeah. She was so responsive, and he suspected she'd spent the last few years hiding that fire.

She moaned.

He deepened the kiss, granting her silent permission to take what she wanted.

Her movements became faster and she ended the kiss before burrowing her head into his shoulder.

"Take it."

She made tiny circular motions against him, getting herself off. He held her, supported her, encouraged her.

She cried out as she convulsed then sank against him.

He let go of her hands and caught her against him. Her breaths came in tiny little gasps.

"How do you keep doing that?" she asked eventually. "An orgasm a week usually keeps me happy. Now I need them every few hours."

Damien stroked the back of her head. "I'll give you as many as you want, Milady."

"You might be creating a monster here, Damien."

"I'm willing to take the chance."

He told her to take as much time as she needed to unpack and settle in while he fetched her remaining items from the car.

Over the years, he'd kept his suite private. But having Catrina here seemed natural and inevitable. He refused to consider how quiet and empty it might seem when she left.

It appeared Gregorio had been in. The empty brandy snifters were gone, and cables protruded through a hole in the desk. She'd be plugged in and ready to work in the morning.

Damien placed her box and computer backpack on her new desk, feeling inordinately pleased with himself.

He rejoined her in the bedroom. She was stowing her bag on a shelf. A few items hung from the hangers. And a drawer stood slightly ajar. He could get used to this. "Can I get you a glass of wine?"

"Not if we're playing."

"We're not."

"Oh?"

"We're listening to music, enjoying the fireplace and seeing where the conversation leads."

"Would you like me to change?"

"No." It was tempting, though. Since he'd packed her suitcase, he knew what was in it. Red leather. A corset that left her breasts bare. Skirts, heels, fishnets. He'd been selective. He'd only chosen his favorites.

But she was fine as she was. The fact that he could see the swell of her breasts and a faint outline of her nipples was enough for now.

"I'm afraid you're confusing me."

"Good."

She followed him back into the living room. He opened a bottle of red for her and set it aside for a few minutes while he adjusted the blinds. She perched on the arm of the couch, watching him, with one leg crossed over the other at the ankle.

He flipped the switch to turn on the fireplace then selected a jazz station on the satellite system.

"Frank Sinatra?" she asked.

"Is that okay?"

"Fine. Just…" She paused and linked her hands on one thigh. "I don't know what I thought you'd choose, maybe classic rock. But not that."

"Were you thinking I'd strip you down, or better yet, dress you up?"

"Actually, yes."

"Maybe shackle your naked body while I arouse you to the point you're begging for release?"

She licked her upper lip. "Well…"

Foreplay took many different forms. "Sit with me?" He'd phrased it as a question, but he knew there'd be no doubt she'd understand it wasn't a request.

He poured them each a glass of wine.

She was on the couch when he turned back around, but she was pressed against the far side.

"We could watch television," she suggested. "A news show. Or surely there's some sporting event on. Or maybe a movie. I'm even up for an action adventure, doesn't have to be a chick flick."

"No."

"No? That was pretty domineering."

"It was," he said unapologetically. "Move a little closer to the middle, if you don't mind." He held out the glass, forcing her to move to accept it.

"I'm on to your nefarious plan," she said when he sat next to her.

"Are you?" He took a drink. "Do tell."

"All this is part of your idea of submission. And it's so different from mine that you're illustrating how complex it is."

"It's part of submission, how?"

She looked at him over the rim of the glass. Her stare was wide and unblinking. "I'm guessing you're going to tell me a true sub doesn't get to hide any part of who they are."

"Well done. And yes, you're right. I want to know all about you. What makes your heart flutter? What things sneak up on you when you're trying to go to sleep?"

"I didn't agree to all this," she said.

"You did. You couldn't have imagined that I'd keep you tied up twenty-four hours a day."

"No?"

"Not that the idea is without merits. I love how your nipples harden when you're anticipating the touch of my leather. But I invited you to explore for a couple of weeks. I didn't invite you to my dungeon for a few random scenes."

"It *is* a nice dungeon," she said lightly.

"I invited you into my life," he said.

The wine sloshed in the glass. He took it from her and slid it onto a nearby table. "And I'm glad you're here," he added. He took her hand, raised it and kissed her. Then, still holding her gaze captive, he gently bit her thumb.

She moaned and closed her eyes. "That's—"

"Just the beginning," he said.

Chapter Eight

And it was.

Damien's words, combined with the delicious twinge from his bite, caused her pussy to tighten. He turned her on in ways no one ever had

She opened her eyes to find him staring not just at her, but seemingly inside her. The intensity of the blue chilled her, as if his eyes were made of ice.

He was breathtakingly handsome, and she itched to pull that leather strip from his hair and run her fingers through its thick length.

As he'd planned, he'd turned her idea of submission inside out then he'd dumped it upside down. He made her question everything she'd thought she knew and had assumed.

She used D/s to keep her emotions separate from those of other people. He used it to pry inside. In ways she could never have imagined, he terrified her.

What happened at the end of the two weeks when she went back to her home in Washington Park? If she gave Damien what he wanted, what he demanded, she'd be stripped bare emotionally.

He'd go on with his life as if this had been nothing more than a diversion.

But what about her?

Even though she'd found him annoying at the time, having him at the dinner with her mother and Milton had made it easier for her. Damien's little touches had helped keep her calm. He'd offered silent strength and support in a way, she supposed, it might happen in a real relationship. Not that she'd had any real experience with that.

They spent the next couple of hours discussing mundane things. She told him about her business, and he answered questions that she'd had while he was talking to her mother and Milton earlier.

When she yawned, he said, "Let's go to bed."

Finally.

"Since I didn't bring you any pajamas, I'll get you a T-shirt."

She felt so off balance it was as if he'd spun the world backwards. Shaken, she left her wine glass on the coffee table.

While he tidied up, she took a shower.

He was holding a towel for her when she stepped out.

"Thank you." She lifted her arms and he wrapped it around her.

It was odd sharing the bathroom, strangely intimate to be brushing her teeth only a few feet from where he stood in front of his own sink.

He'd taken off his shirt, but his hair was still held back. In so many ways, he was right. Part of her had expected him to keep her tied up and to beat her twenty-four hours a day.

His enormous biceps rippled as he moved. She couldn't help but think of the strength he possessed, but also the tenderness he showed her. He restrained his power, she knew. It would have been easy for him to have used too much force with the cane, but he hadn't. Instead, he'd been deliberate with her. Though it had hurt, it had also aroused her.

He grabbed a T-shirt from his closet and held it while she pulled it on. She combed out her hair then braided it while she sat cross-legged on the bed waiting for him.

"Don't think I'm not onto you," he said as he entered the room.

"I'm sorry?" She slid the brush onto the nightstand and scooted against the headboard.

He stood only feet away, arms folded, naked, penis semi-flaccid, legs spread about shoulder-width apart. Though he wore nothing, he looked suitably intimidating.

"Dropping your towel and clothes on the floor and leaving them."

"I apologize. I'm afraid I'm a bit of a slob."

"No you're not. I was in your house, remember? Lived-in with magazines and all kinds of...stuff, but your dirty clothes were in a hamper and all of your toiletries were put away."

"Ah..."

"Point taken. You think I'm a tight-ass."

"It seemed like a better idea ten minutes ago than it does right now," she admitted, her stomach plummeting.

"I think you're hoping for a spanking."

Maybe she had been.

"I'll let you think about it for a while," he said.

"What?"

"Consider your actions carefully, Catrina. We'll talk about it more before we agree on how we handle it."

"About that."

He nodded.

"Can we get it over with?"

"When I say so, yes. Ready for bed?"

She wasn't sure her brain had ever been tied in more knots.

He folded back the comforter then climbed in next to her before turning off the lamp. "Come here," he said.

This was more what she'd expected.

When he pulled her against him and wrapped his arms around her, she said, "There's no lesson for this evening?"

"There definitely was."

"I'm not sure what you're talking about."

"The mundaneness of it all. That's where trust and intimacy are built."

"You frustrate me."

"Milady, the feeling is mutual. Now, rest."

"I don't snuggle, Damien."

"You do now."

"But—"

"Go to sleep."

His grip was unbreakable.

It was only a minute later that she heard the change in his breathing pattern that indicated he was already asleep. How was that even possible?

She tried to sneak away, but his hold tightened.

"Stop," he murmured against her ear. "This is a battle you can't win." To reinforce his point, he put a leg over hers.

Trapped but oddly comforted, she gave in.

It had been a hell of a day, and nothing had gone the way she'd planned, from him dominating her in her house, caning her feet, meeting Milton and introducing Damien to her mother, to spending the evening chatting in front of the fireplace.

And the next morning, when she opened her eyes, she was in the bed alone.

She sat up while she blinked. "I think I'm seeing things," she said. "A Celtic god, maybe." And indeed he did look like that. He'd opened the blinds in the other room and light radiated behind him, making his hair appear darker than ever.

Or maybe that was his clothes.

Black T-shirt, black jeans, black leather belt with a thrilling wink from his silver buckle.

Then she noticed something even more relevant—he was holding two cups of coffee. "Is one of them for me? If so, you've got my undying love and devotion."

"In that case, you can have both."

The mattress sank under his weight as he sat near her. "I didn't know whether to let you sleep or wake you up."

"You made the right choice."

"Thank you."

She let the steam bathe her face before taking the first sip of bliss. "But I guess I think I should be doing that for you."

"If you're up first, you're welcome to. But ensuring your happiness is a priority to me. You matter to me, Catrina."

This man, the complexity of him, was ensnaring her. She told herself to be wary, but he was systematically demolishing her resistance.

"I have a conference call with London in ten minutes. You're welcome to use your office or relax here. I can keep the call on my headset so as to disturb you as little as possible."

"I don't have any calls for a couple of hours," she said.

"Oh, even though this area is soundproof, don't think I won't know if you masturbate."

She hadn't even considered it. Now it was the only thing she could think about.

He grinned then left the room.

Diabolical, frustrating, confounding...Dom. She'd have thrown a pillow after his smug face if she hadn't been afraid of spilling her coffee.

She took a shower to finish waking up and while she was there, soaping her body in the steamy warmth, she thought of him, remembering the way he touched her, tormented her, licked and sucked her pussy until she grabbed his hair and forgot how to breathe. It was tempting to slide her fingers between her folds...

"Don't do it."

"Out!" she yelled as she yanked back the shower curtain.

"I will know," he told her. He shot her a quick grin.

Damn him. Somehow, he would know. Despite his assurances that there were no cameras in the private rooms, she didn't believe him. "Don't you have a call to take, or a company to acquire, something other than bothering me?" She closed the curtain again.

"Beautiful nipples," he said. "Make sure you get them very clean."

She risked a peek and discovered she was all alone.

It took her half an hour to put up her hair, dress and drink a second cup of coffee. All the while, sexual tension gnawed at her. Why the hell hadn't he touched her last night or this morning?

If she were honest, she'd admit she'd had one of the best night's sleep ever.

Changing her mind about her outfit, she went back to her closet. Instead of jeans and a T-shirt, she wore a skirt and heels, stockings and a garter belt.

Before leaving the room, she hung up her towel and put away her discarded clothing.

Fresh cup of coffee in hand, she went into the office.

Her breath froze in her lungs.

Over the years, she'd seen Damien at his sexy best, in leather, in a suit and tie. But nothing had prepared her for this. He stood in front of the monitors. One screen showed a glossy conference room table, presumably in England. The other was filled with the face of an aging, attractive gentleman, his tie loosened and askew. His face was drawn in tight lines that radiated his displeasure.

"I do understand, Malcolm, but that's my best, final offer. Look around you. I think the rest of the board will agree you have no choice but to accept."

A pulse ticked in the other man's temple.

This was Damien at his absolute hottest. Resolved. Unshakable. In control.

Little shivers danced through her.

Now she wished she'd masturbated in the shower, even if she risked his wrath.

She stayed toward the back of the room, out of view as she went to her own desk. Obviously having noticed her, he acknowledged her with a thumbs-up.

Feeling welcomed, she continued on.

While he gave the other man a deadline and ended the call with a series of professional pleasantries, she took her files out of the box and moved them into their temporary drawer.

Gregorio, she assumed, had provided everything else she'd need—a printer, paper, notepads, an assortment of pens, even a purple stapler.

As she was sliding the box out of sight, Damien joined her.

"Everything in order?" he asked.

"Yes, thanks."

"Let Gregorio know if you need anything else. Join me for breakfast?"

"Sounds great."

Downstairs, he made them both omelets and brewed a fresh pot of coffee.

Afterwards, she offered to clean the kitchen. "To make up for the mess I left last night."

"Apology accepted."

"Really?" she asked over her shoulder as she rinsed a plate. He was at the table, long legs stretched in front of him, coffee in hand.

"That doesn't mean I can't or won't deliver a secondary punishment at my discretion."

"I thought the fact you didn't let me masturbate in the shower was your chastisement."

"No. Simply an order because it pleased me. That's my prerogative."

The back door opened, and Gregorio gave a courtesy knock as he entered. "Got coffee?"

This felt so…normal. It occurred to her she'd had no idea what happened at the Den during the week. She'd always figured the two showed up before an event and threw open the door for the debauchery to begin.

"Am I interrupting, Boss?" he asked.

"Come in," Damien invited.

As always, Gregorio radiated sex appeal. Even though it was a Monday, he wore an earring, and he was every bit the rogue in that butter-soft leather jacket. His attire wasn't just an image he projected, it was part of who he was. All in all, this wasn't a bad place to work and spend two weeks.

"Morning, Milady," he said. "I like the fact you look like you could run a company but you're up to your elbow in soap suds."

"Damien cooked. So I'm cleaning."

"I think we have a French maid's outfit in the storeroom," Gregorio told Damien.

"Now there's a hell of an idea."

She dropped the silverware into the basket in the dishwasher with a horrific clatter.

"Bring it up," Damien said.

"No." She held up a hand as she turned to face the men. "Absolutely not."

"Do it," Damien said.

Gregorio grinned, and the motion looked calculatedly diabolical.

"You seem delighted with yourself," she snapped out.

"I'm picturing it right now. My place needs to be dusted."

"Aren't you a switch?" she asked him.

"Oh, yeah."

"Then I'll get even with you for this."

"I'll bare my ass for you, Milady. As long as you don't hit like a girl."

"We can go downstairs anytime." And she would definitely be meting out a punishment and not a pleasure beating.

"Boss?"

Damien put his cup on the table with a firm smack. "Not for the next two weeks."

"Figured." He poured himself a cup of coffee, refilled Damien's, then held up the pot near Catrina, as if it were a peace offering.

"With cream." She dried her hands on a towel. "If you gentlemen will excuse me, I have work to do." She grabbed her cup on the way out of the kitchen.

It took her a few minutes to settle in. The office space pulsed with Damien's presence even though he wasn't in the room.

The exchange with the men had disturbed her even though it shouldn't have. She wore scandalous clothing every time she visited the Den. But she would sub only for Damien.

He returned while she was on a phone call with a client. As he had before, he gave her a silent greeting then went on with his own work.

They lunched together, without Gregorio, then went back upstairs. Being this close to him, hearing the modulated tones of his voice, even if she couldn't make out the exact words, gave her a little thrill.

He looked at her numerous times, not disturbing her, but letting her know he was aware of her.

Mid-afternoon, he approached her desk. "You dressed that way on purpose. After I told you not to play with yourself in the shower."

"Yes," she admitted, looking up at him.

"You wanted my attention."

She nodded.

"What were you hoping I'd do?"

When she moved aside a file, he asked, "Hike up your skirt?"

In instant response, she felt a fluttering in her stomach.

He leaned against the edge of her desk, close, so close, marking her space as his. She smelled his musk, couldn't look away from the laser focus in his eyes.

"Maybe run my hand between your legs?"

She didn't answer.

"Finger your pussy?"

Her mouth dried.

"Maybe fuck you?"

"All of those," she said breathlessly.

He nodded.

This power play did a number on her brain. Never knowing what he'd say, how he'd react or when he'd approach her kept her on edge. She hated it. She was starting to crave it.

"Please stand."

All day, all of last night, nerves had inched through her, forcing her to suppress them.

She rolled back her chair then stood and waited for him to speak again. He crooked his finger then pointed at a spot on the floor right in front of him.

Captivated, she followed his unspoken command.

"I may ban jeans." He lifted the hem of her skirt.

At the barest brush of skin on skin, she moistened.

"Love the stockings," he said. He traced one of the garters upwards, bypassing her pussy to skim her belly.

She could barely breathe.

"You've seduced me all day," he said.

"I've seduced you, Damien?"

"You inspired me to get all my work done fast so that I would have more time with you."

With his free hand, he unbuttoned her shirt and caressed her breasts through her bra. If this was part of submission, she liked it. Her body zinged with anticipation.

He didn't linger anywhere, but he looked at her intently. Motions slow, he moved between her legs. "You can come anytime, Milady."

"I need it," she said.

"I know. I know."

She suspected he really did.

Catrina allowed her head to fall forward to rest on his broad chest. He brought her off, slowly, deliberately.

She cried out as the orgasm snuck up then took her legs out from under her.

He was there to catch her.

Before she knew what was happening, he had her across the desk.

"Grab the other side."

She heard rustling, but when she turned her head, couldn't see what he was doing. He scorched her ass with what had to be his belt.

She screamed.

"There's a price for your torment, Milady."

"I'll gladly pay it, Damien," she said. Anything was better than being ignored. And she knew he hadn't hit hard, just enough to get her attention, but on top of yesterday's caning, it didn't take much to ignite her senses.

"Don't let go," he told her as he striped her again.

The orgasm he'd given her minutes ago hadn't made this any easier. She was aroused and hungry again.

"Your ass is so red, Milady. Made for my belt."

The thick leather felt different than anything else, covering a broader area. She liked it. And she understood better now why her boys asked for certain implements rather than others. Each—his hand, belt, cane, flogger—created a different sting or sear. This suited her.

Swimming through a minefield of sensation, she lost count of the hits and only became aware of the two of them, the numbness of her fingers where she gripped the desk and the dampness of the wood where her tears fell.

She barely registered that it had ended, but she felt his cock at her entrance.

"Say it."

"Fuck me, Damien. Fuck my pussy."

He did, slamming into her with the same ferocity with which he'd beaten her, satisfying the craving he'd created. She came again. Then again as he pulled her hips backward, held her imprisoned and kicked apart her legs a little more.

In that moment, she was his.

She wanted no one else.

Time merged then ceased to exist.

He played with her clit and said, "Squeeze my cock. Come."

She would have insisted she couldn't climax on command, but he surged in her so deeply, she was helpless.

His dick grew harder in her, signaling his impending orgasm.

That, *that* was enough for her to go over the edge again.

He jerked a few times before gasping. He said her name with a guttural moan then ejaculated.

He moved aside her hair to soothe her nape. "You... Milady. Thank you."

She said nothing. She thought of a dozen different things but she couldn't force a single thought to coalesce into the words that would cross her vocal cords.

He helped her to stand and straighten her skirt. He buttoned up her blouse and watched as she tucked it into her waistband.

"Back to work."

"Are you serious?" she asked.

"I have a meeting with Gregorio then I'll take you to dinner. Be ready in an hour. And wear what I leave on the bed for you."

He walked off, presumably to dispose of the condom.

And she sank into her chair.

She needed to find some furniture polish to clean her tears from the desk top. First, she took a long drink of her water.

He dropped a kiss on the top of her head as he walked past.

Telling herself she would survive this, she picked up her phone and called her mother, something she'd put off most of the day.

"How's your young man?" Evelyn asked.

"Damien?" she responded, stalling. How did she answer that question?

"Yes, Damien. How many do you have?"

"He's an acquaintance."

"Right."

"Right?" she repeated.

"Business meetings aren't held on Sundays. And associates don't touch each other the way he touched you. And furthermore," she pronounced with the same flourish as a television lawyer, "you wouldn't have brought him along unless you were in one car, which you wouldn't have been in unless he'd picked you up somewhere."

Catrina's mother was giving her a headache. "He's fine," she said.

"He must be special to you."

Catrina paused. "I have no idea yet. It's nothing serious. I mean that."

"You know, my Cat, you're the one who tells clients it's okay to fall in love again. You even told me that."

Catrina sighed. "It's easier to give advice than to accept it."

"I'm sure you're right."

"But I didn't call to talk about my life."

"Of course not. You called to stick your nose in mine."

"That's not true."

"Look, sweetheart, I realize you think you know best." Evelyn's voice was soothing. "You want to reassure yourself that I'm aware of what I'm doing, but you're positive I don't. I appreciate that you don't want me to get hurt and lose everything again, but honey, that was over twenty years ago."

"I know, but…"

"You took on the burden in ways you never should have. And then when that jackass fiancée of yours did the same things your father did, it reinforced your worldview." Evelyn sighed. "It was a struggle back then, I grant you, and I should have never allowed you to see the struggle."

"Mother, you couldn't have hid it."

"I tried to protect you," Evelyn said. "But I could have done better for you."

She recalled Damien's words. "I think you did okay."

"I wish I could be as sure. But I do know this. Milton makes me laugh. I feel alive more than I ever have. He has plenty of his own money."

"So why do you need to get married?"

"We don't need to. I want to be a bride, and have flowers and a cake." She paused. "I never had them."

Catrina's shoulders slumped forward. "I didn't realize."

Like a schoolgirl, Evelyn giggled. "And I want a honeymoon. Peggy already bought me a negligee."

"Okay, okay. If I don't mention a prenuptial again after this, do you promise not to tell me stuff like that?"

"Oh. Dear. I'm sorry. I was hoping you had a recommendation for a vibrator."

"*Mother.*" She broke the word into two distinct syllables. "Ask Aunt Peggy. I'm sure she knows."

"She recommended two—"

"Exchange financial plans. Make sure your goals align and that you have adequately saved for retirement. Social security will not be enough to keep up with cost of living increases—"

Evelyn's laughter drowned her out.

Finally, Catrina relented.

"Do you know what *you're* doing?"

"I'm afraid I don't have a clue."

"Life is short. Miltey lost his wife a couple of years ago. Don't let fear rob you of possible joy. Be smart, but be happy."

With that, Evelyn said she had to go. Miltey had bought her a gift certificate for a massage, and she had an appointment to use it.

Wondering at the transformation that her mother was undergoing, Catrina disconnected.

She glanced up to see Damien on one of the monitors. He filled an entire screen, and she felt him as keenly as if he were in front of her. He stood in the kitchen, looking directly into the camera. He pointed at his wrist. Even though he didn't wear a watch, she understood his meaning. She was almost out of time. And if there was one thing she'd learnt, it was to take Damien very, very seriously.

* * * *

Over the next few days, they fell into a routine. He brought her coffee in the mornings. They'd work. He'd torment her at some point while they were alone. At night, he'd teach her something new.

Thursday, she drove to Denver and he called to make sure she had made it safely. Rather than chafing at the intrusion, she appreciated it. It was nice to have someone know her comings and goings, even though it meant she was more connected to him.

She met with her client, Lara, and they spent most of the time talking about her soon-to-be ex and her grief. Catrina helped Lara draw up a realistic plan for saving, paying down credit card debt, investing, giving her real tools to use.

"This feels better," Lara said. "It's something I can do other than wring my hands."

In the doorway, Lara hugged Catrina.

She grinned with satisfaction. There was nothing more rewarding than helping others.

It shocked her when she realized her first instinct was to tell Damien about her day. She closed the door and leaned her shoulders against the wood. *Tell Damien?*

In such a short time, he'd become important to her. After her engagement had ended, she'd chosen freedom over intimacy. Now she was questioning that decision. Hating the questions tumbling through her mind, she pushed away from the door.

She straightened her office, realizing she'd definitely been a brat to Damien. So what if he kept his environment in perfect order? He'd made his choices, too. Just because she'd thought his life needed to be shaken up, it didn't mean she had the right to do it.

He'd asked if she thought he was a tight ass.

Maybe he was.

And maybe that restraint was the very thing that attracted her to him.

She sent him a text message, letting him know she was on her way back. And as she slid into the driver's seat, she realized how much she was looking forward to seeing him.

The next afternoon he asked if she'd like to attend the Den's event, stay in their quarters, go out or travel back to his house.

"How about dinner out?" she asked. "Then we can sneak in the back way? I'm not ready to step out in public as your sub."

"Even though you wore a white wristband and scened with me last week?"

"It's different."

He nodded.

"I can't explain it. It just is." When he just looked at her, as if he were unconvinced, she thought it through and added, "Maybe the same reason you didn't want me to play with Gregorio. It's just not… A week ago, things were different."

"They were," he agreed.

"I didn't know how you'd react to seeing me, if the invitation was still open. And now, I don't want to be with anyone else. Unless, of course, it was your choice as part of my training."

His jaw tightened. "It's not."

"Thank you."

He swept back an errant strand of her hair.

As usual, he chose her outfit, this time jeans and a sweater.

"No bra," they said simultaneously.

"A gift arrived for you."

"For me?"

"Get ready to go and meet me in the living room."

Half an hour later, she joined him. He was staring at the fire, an ankle propped on his knee.

He stood the moment she walked in.

No matter where or when, he treated her as if he was glad to see her. She appreciated that more and more.

"You look beautiful, as always, Milady."

"Thank you, Damien."

"Come here, please."

She recognized that tone. He had something planned, but it wouldn't do her any good to ask what it was. Rather than raw nervousness assailing her, curiosity tripped through her.

"Lift your shirt and show me your tits."

She did.

He pulled out a pair of unusual-looking clamps.

"Your gift," he said. "Nipple jewelry."

The small hearts were pretty, and she suspected they'd stay in place just fine. They weren't meant to inflict discomfort like some clamps, but rather, she suspected, meant to be a constant pressure.

"Present your breasts to me, Milady."

She did as he instructed, lifting them toward him.

"I'll be cutting dinner short tonight."

His hoarse admission delighted her. She loved knowing she affected him as much as he affected her.

He sucked on each nipple to distend them before attaching each heart.

"How does that feel?"

"I know they're there," she said. "But not bad."

"Let's go before I end up taking you to bed without feeding you."

At the restaurant, he ordered a bottle of champagne.

"Are we celebrating something?"

"I made a deal with the firm in England."

"Congratulations."

The bottle arrived and she toasted his success.

They each enjoyed a steak dinner, and she was debating whether or not to order dessert when he said, "Get the chocolate cake. You'll need your energy."

The combination of his words and the nipple jewelry put her on the edge of her seat.

When the server returned, he ordered the chocolate cake and offered coffee.

"Just the cake," Catrina said. When they were alone, she added, "I don't want to linger. I'm anxious to go home."

"So you don't want to go to a movie?" he teased. "Maybe dancing? Ice skating?"

"No."

He smiled. "Ah. This must be about your nipples and state of arousal? How does the jewelry feel?"

"Even though the pressure isn't terrible, they're starting to drive me crazy." As if he didn't know it.

"I like looking at the outline, and I like you putting up with them because I requested it."

"Requested?"

"You're always free to refuse."

She was discovering that she liked pleasing him, and she knew he went out of his way to make sure she was happy in return.

He took care of the bill then escorted her outside. He opened her car door then said, "Wait." He slid his hand inside her lapels and flicked at the hearts.

She hissed.

"Milady," he said, indicating she should get in the car.

Catrina wasn't sure if he had been trying to teach her the importance of reaching out to her subs before the scene. But now she understood it on a whole new level.

All afternoon, with his words, his actions, the way he mixed in serious conversation with smoldering, blunt sex talk banked the embers of desire. He stoked it along the way so that when he finally touched her, need flared until it consumed her.

"I've been thinking about having you naked all day."

"Me, too," she replied, looking at him.

Everything he did—from driving, to running a corporation, to dominating her—exuded his controlled power. Experiencing it turned her on.

They returned to the Den with only the valet noting their arrival. The man gave a quick salute, acknowledging Damien as he pulled into the garage.

He put a hand on her shoulder to stop her from getting out of the car. "Show me your breasts."

The unexpected way he issued commands always startled her. She was certain he did it on purpose to keep her guessing. Knowing there was a houseful of people only feet away increased her tension.

Her hand trembled as she pulled apart the knot in her coat belt.

Damien stood close, not helping, just watching as she followed his order.

She lifted her shirt, and the cool air chased goosebumps up her body.

"Even better than I imagined," he said. He squeezed her nipples.

She winced.

"How do they feel now?"

"Achy." It would have been impossible for her to have worn actual clamps the entire evening. As it was, the dull, throbbing pain had distracted her. But this was different, it was actual discomfort. "That hurt."

"Do you want me to take them off?"

Her shirt still raised, she looked up at him and knew this was another lesson. "If that's your pleasure."

"Oh, damn, Milady. Well done."

He released his grip on her nipples. Pain ricocheted through her, leaving her pussy wet and anxious.

"Leave the hearts in place." Then he added, "Put your shirt back down."

She exhaled but didn't protest. While she would have liked to remove the jewelry, submitting to his will gave her pleasure.

He opened the door to the back stairs, and she preceded him up.

"Have you ever been fucked up the ass, Milady?"

She gripped the banister tight to avoid tripping up the stairs.

"I mean before tonight?"

Looking over her shoulder, she said, "No."

"Then I look forward to being your first."

Her whole body felt shaky as she entered their rooms.

"You'll find lube under the sink in the bathroom, along with condoms," he said after he flipped the switch to turn on the fireplace. "There's also a butt plug in the top drawer in my closet. Put it in. That will be the only thing you'll be wearing when you return to me."

When she didn't reply, he asked, "Are my instructions clear?"

"Yes," she whispered. She cleared her throat and said again, "They are."

"First, your nipples."

She took off her coat and draped it over the back of the couch. Then she took off her shirt and dropped it.

"Maybe I'll make you keep them on. I love the way they look."

"Of course, Damien. Your choice."

"Come here."

When she stood in front of him, he closed his fingers around them.

"I wouldn't do this with actual clamps…"

She looked at him.

Rather than releasing each, he pulled them off simultaneously.

She yelped.

"Just as gorgeous." He curled his palms around her breasts then sucked on the peaks to help ease the sting. "Perfect," he said a moment later.

Even though the hearts were gone, a tenderness remained.

"Now, go." He nodded, and she turned from him.

Near the bedroom doorway, the sound of his voice made her freeze.

"Stay there until I say otherwise. I like that view of you with no shirt, jeans, the way your hair hangs down your back." He sucked in a breath. "Everything about you does it for me, Catrina."

She glanced over her shoulder, even though she knew that might incur his displeasure. "You do it for me, Damien."

"Get on with it, Milady. I'm growing impatient."

Images and thoughts crowded her mind as she went into his closet. At her house, he'd had no qualms about going through her clothing, but entering his closet and rifling through his drawers seemed overly personal.

It wasn't just a drawer. It was a treasure trove. Clamps, floggers, even a vibrator. Toward the back, she found the small plug and her breaths came closer and closer together.

In her closet, she finished undressing before going into the bathroom with the glass piece. It took her several tries to insert the slippery thing, and she was ultra-aware of its presence, shifting in her as she moved.

Carrying the lube and a condom, she returned to him.

Damien was seated on the couch, one arm across the back. To her he was devastating.

As always, being nude while he was fully clothed reminded her of her submission, as she was sure he'd intended.

He stood. His cock was already hard, and the sight of it made her mouth dry.

"Bend over. Let me see your plug."

She turned away from him, spread her legs and grabbed her ankles. Her hair fell everywhere. Knowing that he was looking at her made her feel empowered, something she'd never expected to feel as a submissive.

He'd been right that there was much more to it than she'd ever considered.

"That's better than I could have imagined," he said. "And what I imagined was pretty damned good. Now, reach back and spread your buttocks so I can see it better."

Keeping her balance, glad she'd kept up her morning routine of yoga stretches, she did as he requested.

"Exquisite."

For long seconds, silence pulsed.

"Good. Now get on the coffee table. On all fours."

He offered his hand for assistance.

Feeling exposed, she did as he'd said. He circled her several times. She forced herself to stay where she was.

"Those hearts would add to this experience." He crouched in front of her. "What do you say?"

"Your choice, Damien."

Without her knowledge, he'd had them in hand the whole time. She sucked in tiny gasps of air when he closed the jewelry on her already-swollen nipples.

"I may buy you a dozen different sets," he said.

He squeezed her breasts, but even the lightest of touches drove her wild.

Damien left her, then she felt fingertips skimming her spine. He massaged her buttocks and the motion shifted the plug. She moaned.

Then he was everywhere. He played with her pussy, spanked her ass lightly then reached beneath her to toy with the hearts.

She forgot to be nervous and gave herself over to him, becoming more and more aroused.

"You like this, Milady? Getting all my attention, knowing that what I'm doing is for you?"

"Thank you," she said.

He moved behind her. She heard his belt, the rasp of his zipper, the thud of his shoes being tossed on the hardwood.

She swayed, shifting the plug, making her impatient with greed.

"Are you ready for me, Catrina?"

"I've been ready," she said.

He chuckled, the sound deep and rich.

She felt him at the entrance of her pussy. "Damien?"

He slid his thick cock into her, and the sensation of him drove her mad. With the pressure from the plug, she felt overwhelmed.

Relentless, he played with the plug.

She dropped her head to the table, changing the angle, alleviating some of the pressure.

"Back into position, Milady."

"I'm…" She wasn't sure her arms would support her.

He placed his forearm beneath her chest, helping her. "That's how I want you. Understand?"

She nodded.

He thrust his hips, filling her pussy over and over. She thrashed her head. "I'm going to come," she said.

"Not yet."

"This is…" She put all her concentration into thinking about him and ignoring the tension in her lower body. "Too much, Damien."

"You're okay, Milady."

She drank strength from his words.

He kept it up, and she fought off the orgasm. She was dazed, lost when he pulled back.

"Relax."

He tugged on the plug.

The damn thing seemed stuck in there.

"It's coming out, Milady. It will hurt less if you stop the struggle."

Intellectually she understood what he said, but she still tightened her buttocks against the discomfort.

"Put your head down."

Which raised her rear higher.

He slapped both her butt cheeks hard, pitching her forward, and he plucked out the plug while she was distracted.

"That wasn't so bad, was it?"

Then before she knew what was happening, his cockhead was pushing into her ass.

"Good God!"

"You're okay. You can move around if you need to."

She panted and tried to get away as he rocked, entering her deeper and deeper. "This isn't fun."

"Almost there," he promised, soothed.

Lied.

It seemed to take him forever to get his cock all the way in her. She couldn't breathe, couldn't think.

Finally, he had her imprisoned.

"You okay?"

"I…" She was. Now that he'd claimed her, she was better.

"So, so tight, Milady. Now, I want you to kneel up."

"You can't be serious."

"I am."

Because he was so strong, he was able to reach around her. His arm was like a band around her chest as he lifted her upper body.

As he moved her, his cock went deeper and deeper, stretching her impossibly wide. "I can't!"

"You did," he said, kissing the side of her neck.

"Damien, it's too much."

"You can safe word, or you can work through it. Either way is fine."

He spoke against her ear, the words a soft, wonderful reassurance. If he thought she could do it, she'd try.

Her forehead drenched in sweat, she nodded.

"Good girl. Now put your hand behind my neck."

"I'm not a contortionist."

"You don't need to be. I've got you."

She couldn't believe this. She was on her knees on the table with Damien supporting her weight in a way that seemed to defy gravity. Her motions slow, she arched her back so that she could do as he said.

Each bit she moved stretched her anus farther apart.

"That's it, Milady."

She squeezed her eyes shut. "It's overwhelming."

"It's supposed to be."

The pressure on her nipples magnified everything else. She was shattering.

"You okay?"

"I'm dying," she said, panting.

"I'll take that as a yes," he replied. Once he was buried as deep as he could go in her ass, he bent his knees so he could move inside her.

She cried out as he drove in again and again. She couldn't think. Perspiration drenched her and the whole while, he had her, possessed her. She'd never felt anything like it. "Do me," she pleaded.

"My absolute pleasure."

He pulled back until the only part inside her was his cockhead then he surged forward again. She screamed. "More," she urged.

"Yes."

He drove into her with the force she wanted.

"Amazing," she said. "It's…"

"I want you to come."

He fingered her clit. Bucking, she pitched forward. Damien pulled her upright, holding her. He groaned and ejaculated in spurts.

The change in pace, the way he touched her and the swelling of his cock were a lethal combination. She muttered things that were incomprehensible as she came.

Damien continued to support her as his cock softened. She'd never felt more connected to anyone. "I had no idea," she said.

Slowly he lowered her to the table's surface.

He withdrew his cock then picked her up and carried her toward the master en suite. As he strode, she rested her cheek against his chest. Lesson learned. After their time together, she'd never again be the same.

But with the way he looked at her, she knew he wasn't done with her yet.

Chapter Nine

"Before you get started, I'd like you to change."

Catrina looked across the table at him. "Did you have something in mind?"

Over the nearly two weeks they'd spent together, they'd fallen into a routine. When they ate at home, he did the cooking. She would pull up a barstool and keep him company unless she was working.

Afterwards, she'd load the dishwasher and wipe the counters while he put away the leftovers. They made an effective team.

He splashed a little more red wine in each glass. "I left an outfit for you in the powder room."

"Really?"

"Go see."

Her eyebrows knitted in a serious frown, she rose. She returned less than a minute later.

"Are you serious?" she demanded, shock echoing through her words.

"Totally," Damien assured her, pushing back his chair.

"This is a French maid's outfit," she said, holding up the frothy black fabric.

"It is indeed."

Indignant, with one hand on her hip, she'd never looked more appealing.

"There's nothing wrong with what I'm wearing."

"You're right. In fact, it's lovely." He enjoyed seeing her in skirts and stilettos. "But this is my choice for tonight. And I suggest you put it on in the next two minutes unless you want to wear it all day, every day for the remainder of your time here."

"I don't understand why I'm being punished for something I apologized for a week ago."

"Milady, you left a coffee cup, complete with a nasty ring, on my desk this morning. It was all but glued on there when I moved it an hour ago."

"That doesn't count."

"No?"

"You're going to hold that against me?" She sighed. "You're the one who bothered me while I was looking out of the window. And you got a blowjob out of it."

"I do like the way you give head."

"Then…"

"Put the outfit on, Catrina."

"Be reasonable."

"A reddened ass would go nicely with that outfit."

"You're a beast."

"Diabolical," he agreed. "One minute."

Her shoes were an angry tattoo against the floorboards as she strode away. He took a sip from his wine. This was going to be a hell of a show.

It was almost two minutes later when he heard her footfall. This time, she came toward him with a soft, sultry walk that made his cock instantly hard. She'd fluffed her hair, tied the apron way too tight, skipped the matching thong and tightened the satin laces on the top so tight that her cleavage looked twice its normal size. She had a black fabric collar tied around her throat. He had to wonder who was being mastered.

She exaggerated every movement.

"Hello, Master," she said. "How can I please you?"

He rolled the wine glass between his palms. This might not have been one of his better ideas.

Catrina moved behind him. The hairs on his nape stood up in response to the stir of her breath. Then she stuck out her tongue, nipped his flesh then laved the hurt.

If she kept this up, the kitchen would never get clean.

Which could lead to punishing her in the morning.

"May I, Sir?"

She brushed her breasts against his upper arm as she took away his plate.

Within a minute, his cock throbbed.

She reached across the table for her dishes, exposing her bare bottom.

"Think carefully about what you're doing, Milady."

"Oh, yes, Sir. Thank you for the advice, Sir."

God, he loved how that rolled off her tongue. Now, if only she'd say it when she wasn't teasing.

She took her time doing the dishes, bending over to pick up some unseen item from the floor, making sure she wiggled her hips as she moved each plate from the sink to the dishwasher.

Watching her was delicious torture.

After she'd cleared the table, she returned with a damp towel.

"Pardon my reach, Sir." She leaned across him and wiped the table. Twice.

Finally, unable to take it, he pulled her off her feet and settled her in his lap, facing him.

"Oh, no, Sir!" She wiggled as she straddled him. "Are you going to have your wicked way with me?"

"I'm afraid so, Milady." He maneuvered them so that she was sitting and he was standing. He kicked off his shoes, socks and pants then grabbed a condom from his wallet.

He sheathed his already-hard dick.

She licked her upper lip.

He throbbed.

"But what of my virtue?" she asked.

"Milady, when I'm done with you, your lack of virtue will be the least of your worries."

He picked her up, sat and pulled her down on his cock. She was already wet, and her pussy welcomed him with a tight squeeze.

"Oh, sweet God," she whispered.

"Ride me."

She moved on him, raising and lowering herself. He groaned. His little vixen had turned the tables.

He yanked open her front laces and palmed her breasts, lifting them so he could suck her distended nipples.

Catrina pulled the leather strip from his hair and dug her fingers in, pressing against the back of his head, holding him tight as she fucked him.

He pressed a finger against her anal whorl and slowly worked his way inside. She groaned and lifted up, giving him greater access.

She said his name a dozen times, turning it into a chant.

He made sure he gave her an orgasm before he reached his climax, but damn, it took everything he had to hold back as long as he did. He could have come the first time she lowered herself on him.

"Well, Sir, that was unexpected."

"Let that be a lesson to you," he said sternly.

She pulled back his head so she could look at him. "Why, yes, Sir. Of course, Sir." Then she kissed his forehead before scampering off his lap and heading upstairs.

It was then that he realized she'd left him with the remainder of the clean-up. Including her discarded clothes in the powder room.

Yep. He'd definitely showed her who the Dom was in this relationship.

* * * *

Two cups of coffee in hand, Catrina stopped in the doorway of the office space she shared with Damien. Greedily, she watched him. He was on his headset, pacing. His hair was loose, long, rakish.

She didn't get tired of seeing him like this, in charge with his take-control power radiating, affecting everything and everyone in his orbit.

Including her.

Including her? *Especially* her.

His T-shirt showed his biceps, and damn, had he poured himself into those jeans?

Seeming to sense her, like he always did, he pivoted.

Even though he was in the middle of a conversation, he beckoned her in, indicating she should sit on his desk.

He walked over to accept the coffee she offered, and he pulled out his earpiece long enough to place a gentle kiss on the top her head.

Since her first meeting wasn't for another thirty minutes and they'd both worked late the evening before, she decided to wait while he finished his call. She wasn't sure what was being discussed, but the financial planner in her was intrigued by the word *millions,* particularly when it was followed by *dollars.*

He was nodding in response to something being said, and she sipped her coffee. The blinds were open, letting in the dappled sunlight. The screens showed only the outdoor cameras, a blanket of snow on the trees and grounds. Steam rose from the hot tub. A deer wandered just outside a fence.

Such a peaceful, wonderful place.

Saying goodbye in a couple of days was going to break her heart. Not only did she love the Den, but she enjoyed his company every evening as they sat on the couch, music in the background, a fireplace glowing. Sharing the day's events with another person was something she'd never experienced before. Even when he pried more information out of her than she liked, it was nice talking to someone who was supportive and non-judgmental.

The idea of leaving here—and him—ached like a physical pain.

Catrina breathed in and reminded herself to keep her emotional distance. She'd known from the start this was a temporary arrangement, orchestrated to teach her some things about submission.

She shoved away the nagging whisper that it might already be too late.

He hung up and strode to her. He put his cup on the desk and plucked hers from her hand to put it next to his.

"Time to say good morning to my lovely sub." He linked his arms around her and pulled her up until she was barely inches from him.

She tipped back her head to look at him. "I'm not sure what you're thinking," she said. "But I'm not sure I like it."

"How do you know?"

"Because you are looking down your nose and you appear very serious. So your head is either still thinking about business or you're considering doing something wicked to me."

"Wicked," he said. "You're onto me."

"Ah."

"Hold out your tongue."

She blinked.

"Don't make me repeat myself." The teasing was gone from his voice, replaced by a stern, wouldn't-tolerate-disagreement tone.

"I'm not sure I want to."

"No?" He pulled her a little closer. His cock pressed against her.

Her resolve wavered. "It will hurt."

"Are you sure?"

The question piqued her interest, as she was sure he'd intended.

If she'd had any doubts before about Damien Lowell's ability to master her, it was gone now. He knew exactly how to get her to do what he wanted.

Butterflies doing a backstroke in her bloodstream, she stuck out her tongue. Before he could touch her, she chickened out.

"Catrina," he snapped.

"Sorry." She obeyed his command but closed her eyes.

He gently held the tip of her tongue.

It was everything she could do not to dance away.

When he increased the pressure, she whimpered, not from pain but from the raw pulse of desire.

Damien took one of her hands and placed it on the front of his trousers. She squeezed his cock as she surrendered and leaned into him.

Time was swallowed by sensation.

She barely registered the way he decreased the pressure until he sucked her tongue into his mouth. Then it became a kiss that left her raw, ragged and breathless.

When he finally ended it, setting her away from him, she couldn't hold up her head.

"Thanks for the coffee, Milady. Now get to work."

She shook her head and looked at him. "Seriously? That's it?"

"It's a work day. What else did you expect?"

"You to finish what you start," she said. She continued to stroke him, certain he was joking. "It will only take a minute for both of us to be satisfied."

He clamped a hand around her wrist, stilling her movements. "You'll have to wait until tonight."

"You're the most frustrating man I've ever met."

"It's my decision."

She tried one more angle. "I'd focus better if I had an orgasm."

"This way you'll also be thinking about tonight. I'd like you to meet me downstairs after dinner."

"Oh?"

"That was foreplay, Milady, not a tease."

He moved her hand to her side before letting it go. "Yes…Damien." It would have been easy to call him Sir. In fact, not using the title was becoming more difficult. She was thinking of him in those terms, but actually saying it would mean she'd accepted his domination.

The night she'd dressed in the French maid's get-up, she'd been free to use the word without either of them taking it too seriously. It had felt liberating.

"Don't even think of using a vibrator," he said as he let her go.

"But…"

"Please honor my request."

The morning dragged. "I'm not sure I like your idea of foreplay," she said over lunch.

"That's good to know."

He gave her a quick kiss before excusing himself to return to work. She sank against her chairback and blew out a breath, ruffling her hair.

Gregorio knocked then entered without waiting for an invitation. He brushed snow from his sleeves before hanging up his black leather jacket.

What was it with the men and leather around here?

"Where's the boss?"

"Back at work."

"Everything okay?" He helped himself to a cup of coffee. "Yuck," he said.

"Been there a while."

"What, since the turn of the century?" He put it in the microwave and pulled out a carton of cream. "So, dish, Milady. What's up? It's not like you to sulk."

She thought about denying it, but figured that would do no good. "Damien can be confounding."

"Submission challenges?"

"I think I'll stick with being a Domme."

"Really?" The microwave dinged and he took out the cup. He added a dollop of cream, tasted it again, then added another drop.

"Is that a coffee or a latte at this point?"

"Neither. Putting it in the java family is an insult."

"Want me to brew you another pot?"

"Thought you were done being a sub?"

"Damien is clear about common courtesy and D/s."

He dragged back a chair and sat across from her. "You're a quick study. So. I imagine this has been a challenge for you. Confusing?"

"Yeah. I knew I wasn't a sub. And a whole lot of the time has been instructive."

"But?"

"I like Damien, okay?" She grabbed Gregorio's cup and took a drink, more because she wanted something to do with her hands than anything else.

"And that's a problem because…"

"I'm a Domme. And sometimes he pisses me off enough to want to bend him over and blister his ass."

"You're horny."

She blinked. "What?"

"Deny it." He took back his coffee.

"So?"

"It's a hell of a journey," he said. "I don't blame you for finding it confusing."

"The submission part, I get. Or at least I think I do. He was right that I'll be a better Domme when this is over."

"And the rest?"

"Sitting with him on the couch." She paused. "At night. The talking. Maybe a movie. It's…intimate. Not sex, but sharing things, even seemingly insignificant details. I've never had anything like it. I'm going to miss it, even though I never knew I wanted it."

"Who says you have to give it up?"

"Do you see Damien keeping me around when this is done? If I want to meet him as an equal?"

"You're still seeing a submissive as someone less important or inferior to a Dom?"

"I didn't say that."

"Didn't you?"

She brushed her hair back from her face.

"Discuss this with Damien. I'd give you my opinion, but you need to hear it from him." When she didn't respond, he added, "If that intimacy thing you're talking about is real, then you'll trust him enough to go to him. Tell him what's on your mind. Listen to what he has to say. He could want the same things as you. You could work out a compromise."

"How do two dominants have a relationship?"

"Unless they discuss that, they don't." He took back his cup and swallowed a drink from it. "Tastes like shit."

"Dump it out."

"It's caffeine, and I had a long night."

"Doing what?"

"None of your business."

"I should be with you. I could flog you every night."

"Not on my watch," Damien said.

She froze at the chill in his voice.

Gregorio shrugged. "Security cameras, Milady."

"It was a joke," she said, turning to look at Damien, her heart thundering at double time. She stood, met his gaze, silently implored him to understand. "Since Gregorio is a switch... I'm babbling."

"Go on."

"I was telling him about my frustrations over the last few days." She dropped her gaze. "Sorry if I was out of line."

"You're an adult, Milady. You can discuss anything you want with anyone you wish. I'd like it if you would come to me."

"After lunch, I tried."

"So you're complaining to Gregorio you're sexually frustrated because I wouldn't get you off upstairs?"

"God. No." Exasperated, she took a step toward him. "It's about me. My confusion."

"Fears?"

"Yes."

"I'm glad you talked to Gregorio. And I want you to know that I'm available to listen, too. I may be a caveman, but if you whack me up the side of the head, you can get my attention." He took the final step that would bring them within inches of each other then he took hold of her upper arms with the reassuring gentleness that could only come from such strength. "I have broad shoulders, Milady. To help carry whatever troubles you have."

"That's what I told her."

"You..." He addressed Gregorio over his shoulder. "I thought we had a one o'clock meeting?"

"I'm here, Boss."

Damien jerked his head toward the back stairs.

"Oh. Right. I'll be waiting in your office." He picked up his coffee cup then headed up.

"To be fair," she said when they were alone, "Gregorio did tell me to talk to you."

"I believe him. And you. As long as you're here as my sub you scene with no man but me. If that's not acceptable, we can discuss it. But you're not free to scene with others without first seeking permission."

"Were you listening, Damien? It was a joke." Her voice was higher pitched than normal, and she closed her eyes to get hold of her fraying temper. When she did, she hit them both with the raw truth. "I don't want to be with anyone but you."

"Good." He loosened his grip and he made tiny circles with his fingers. "I appreciate you saying so." He dragged her onto her toes. "We have a lot to talk about tonight."

"Yes," she agreed. "We do."

He eased her toward him and his thick cock pressed against her.

"What about the security cameras?" she reminded him.

"There's no volume unless I turn it up."

"But we are providing a peep show."

"Come here."

He led her into the powder room.

"A clandestine meeting, Damien?"

He spun her around so fast her breath whooshed out. She desperately pushed her hands flat against the wall as he lifted her skirt and blasted her with five hot slaps on her rear. Then he yanked aside her thong and masturbated her until she screamed out an orgasm and collapsed in a sobbing heap against the wall.

It may have taken him ten seconds to give her the relief she'd all-but begged for.

His motions now tender, he turned her back to him and held her tight against his chest. In his arms, she shook. Damien didn't let her go until she found the wherewithal to push him away.

"I needed that," she admitted.

"I know." He took a washcloth from a drawer and daubed her face. "Better, Milady?"

"Much." She gave him a smile. "Thank you." But she was lying. And she wondered if he knew it.

Conflicted, she followed him from the room.

The restless energy that had been churning all day worsened during the afternoon. The scene with Damien should have soothed her, but it didn't. In fact, it contributed to her cauldron of angst. She craved his touch, didn't want this to end, couldn't figure out a way for it to last. The more often they scened, the deeper she cared for him. The more they shared, the more she ached to share.

Trying to work was impossible, and being separated from him and Gregorio by only a glass partition was torture.

Unable to concentrate, restless, she went into the suite and grabbed her coat from the closet. "I'm going for a walk," she told Damien.

"Would you like me to go with you?"

"No problem," Gregorio said, pushing back his chair. "We can finish up at a more convenient time."

"Thanks, but I'd rather be alone."

She walked for less than an hour. Her toes were numb in her boots, her fingers were frozen even though she'd kept them in her pockets and she was grateful her hair covered her ears. As it was, the cold bit at her lobes.

The physical exercise did little to relieve her tension.

When she entered the kitchen, Damien was standing in front of the stove, whisking something in a pan. "Right on time," he said.

"Security cameras?" she guessed. "That's how you knew I was on my way back. You were watching me?"

"You were always in my sight."

"I don't know whether to be relieved or freaked out."

"Grateful," he suggested. "If you'd had any troubles, I'd have found you. And I knew when to have the hot chocolate ready."

"Hot chocolate?" She stamped the snow off her feet, hung up her coat then wandered across the room. "With milk?"

"Of course."

She glanced around. "Where's the little packages?"

"I'm insulted," he said.

"Why?"

"It's homemade. Milk, cocoa powder, sugar, a pinch of salt."

"No packages?" she asked again.

"No packages," he confirmed.

"Homemade?" she repeated.

"With whole milk."

Little things like this were why she was falling for him. "I'm salivating."

"Have a seat at the table. I'll bring you a mug."

"Is Gregorio gone?"

"Yes. He and I will finish up tomorrow." He filled two mugs.

Catrina sat in her usual chair. It struck her that they'd spent enough time together to develop a routine, patterns. And always, she was on Damien's right hand side.

"You didn't have to do this," she said as he slid a yellow ceramic mug in front of her. Gratefully, she wrapped her cold hands around it and lifted it close to her face. "But I'm glad you did. It smells divine." She breathed in the rich, chocolate scent. "Thank you."

"A Dom takes care of his sub, always."

She looked up at him. He'd remained standing.

"It's a responsibility I take seriously."

When she didn't respond, he added, "One I'm honored to have."

Again, he'd taught her a lesson. Being a dominant was about more than meeting someone's physical needs. Emotions and feeling could create a ball of complication that took time and energy to work through. And he not only seemed to feel obligated, but also compelled to untangle the mess. No relationship with a man, ever, had coaxed her to commit to that type of energy.

"I didn't mean to interrupt your afternoon's work," she said.

He took a chair, turned it backwards and straddled it as he faced her. "The schedule can be rearranged. Whatever is bothering you needs to be discussed."

She took a drink of her chocolate. "It's amazing." Rich and creamy, warming her from the inside.

"Talk to me," he encouraged her.

"I'm sure Gregorio filled you in."

"Not at all. This is between us, Milady. Gregorio is loyal to a fault. To both of us."

"I don't know what to say," she admitted, repeatedly tracing the handle, stalling. If she had wanted to talk about this with him, she would have already done so. "This experience has been so much more than I could have imagined. Thank you for it. You're right. I'll be a much better Domme. I guess part of me isn't ready for it to be over."

"We're not done yet."

"I know." That frightened her the most. It was already becoming difficult to imagine life without him. And she was determined to be self-sufficient.

"We have an appointment in the dungeon," he reminded her.

"I didn't forget."

"And a weekend ahead of us."

She told herself to enjoy the moment rather than living in the future.

"Would you like to go out to dinner?"

"Do we have any leftovers? I think the hot chocolate has spoiled my appetite. And yeah, my mother taught me better."

"We can start our play earlier that way," he said. "If you're hungry afterwards, we can go out to dinner then. This afternoon, I prefer you naked."

The way he lowered his eyelids slightly as he looked at her and reached across to tuck the hair behind her ears made her thought process scramble.

Common sense urged her to run away, but a stronger compulsion forced her to stay.

He made dinner while she set the table.

They worked in tandem, already having learned to anticipate the other's needs.

Generally the conversation flowed, but not tonight. He seemed to be giving her long spaces in case she wanted to fill the silence. Since she really didn't know how to say what was on her mind, she remained silent and picked at her food, using the hot chocolate as an excuse not to eat.

When the kitchen was clean, he said, "Would you still like to meet downstairs? I'm happy to take you out, maybe to a movie? A night club? Bowling?"

"Bowling?"

"Thought I'd see if you were paying attention."

"My average is ninety-nine," she said. "So I only go with girlfriends and mainly for the beer."

"We could hang out upstairs if you prefer."

"No." She shook her head. Talking was the last thing she wanted to do. "I'd prefer to play, if you would."

"Ten minutes? Be waiting on your knees in the third room on the left."

She frowned. "That's the one with the St. Andrew's cross."

"It is. You ever been on one?"

"Of course not."

"Sublime experience. You'll enjoy it."

The idea of being spread wide and attached to the wooden structure shaped like an X sent a jolt through her. And if it hadn't, the look on his face would have.

"Time is ticking, Milady. You'll want to be ready when I get there."

She didn't need to be told a second time.

It felt odd to be walking through the Den by herself. Without dozens of people around, the rooms seemed extra-large, and her footsteps echoed hollowly.

She descended the stairs and made her way to the room he'd indicated. She took in the St. Andrew's cross and something odd happened inside. Anxiousness drifted away, leaving her strangely relaxed. When she'd arrived almost two weeks ago, his orders had made her nerves taut. Now they settled her.

After taking off her clothes and folding them neatly, she knelt. Her hearing was attuned for sounds of him. And because of the home's emptiness, she was aware of each step that brought him closer to her.

Catrina spread her knees apart and put her hands behind her neck. As he entered, she lowered her gaze to the floor.

"Damn, woman, no one would know you weren't a sub. You look perfect there." He walked around her. "Very pleasing, Milady."

"Thank you, Damien."

"It's difficult at times to play with you. I'd rather fuck you."

She looked up. "That would be okay, too," she said.

"Onto the cross."

The structure seemed more imposing than it did when she affixed subs to it. "Which direction?" she asked. Nerves unexpectedly skittered through her as she wondered what he had planned. So much for feeling settled.

"Facing me."

She'd been afraid of that.

He made quick work of securing her wrists and ankles.

"I'm going to introduce you to the crop."

"Good thing you tied me up before you said that."

"Scared?"

"Should I be?"

"Yes."

Her stomach dropped.

"You have your safe word."

She nodded.

Damien made a show of rolling back his cuffs. She wanted to look away, but instead, she was transfixed.

She tracked his every motion as he crossed to the wall and selected a crop with a large flapper. "This is going to hurt," she said.

"I'm sure it will."

"Could we trade it in for a flogger?"

"Have you ever used one on a sub's testicles?"

"Once."

"Then you should know what it feels like. How it can feel like a feather and how it can sear and how to mix it up for maximum effect."

With the way she was facing, it meant he intended to use it on her most delicate places.

He tested the length, sending it whistling through the air.

She gasped.

"You'll start infinitely soft. You can increase a bit, but on sensitive areas, you need to exercise exquisite control. But your nipples can take more than you might think. And so can your pussy."

She shrank back.

"Shall we start with your pussy?"

Catrina licked her lower lip.

"Milady?"

The word halt ran through her mind, but it didn't come out of her mouth.

He laid the crop's length against his calf. "Look at me. Not it. At me."

She did.

"There are things you need to be cautious with when you're in charge. But have you ever known me to give you more than you can bear?"

She shook her head.

"Then when you're ready, ask for the first blow."

"I'm scared."

"How can I help?"

"Kiss me?" The request shocked her. She wasn't a woman who asked for anything, especially comfort.

But he responded instantly. With a smile, he took a few steps toward her and wrapped his hand in her hair. He angled her head back. "My pleasure."

He gave her the gentlest of kisses, pulled away, let her catch her breath, then leaned in again. Over the course of twenty or thirty seconds, he played with her, teasing, taking more, offering more.

Forgetting her fear, she kissed him back, meeting the thrust of his tongue, then opening her mouth when he plundered the depths.

She wanted to put her arms around him, but he had her trapped. The kiss lasted forever and with her surrender, she said the things she couldn't out loud.

"Shall we get on with it?" he asked as he ended the kiss.

"Will you fuck me after?"

"You can count on it, Milady. I've desired you all day."

"I'm ready," she said.

He ran his palm over the crown of her head. "You please me. Again and again."

For those words, she'd do anything.

He moved away. She realized her back was arched. His kiss had reassured her to the point she was more placid, no longer shrinking in her bondage. Instead, she was allowing the straps to support her weight.

"The crop has a long rod. That can serve the same function as a cane. Be ultra-careful with the way you use it. I'm not saying you can't use it anywhere, but you'd better know what you're doing, how your sub is doing and how much force you're using. If they're flying, it's even more incumbent on you to use caution. The flapper, on the other hand…"

He trailed the leather down her chest, between her breasts, then lower, over the slight swell of her stomach.

She tensed before he hit her. But when it was over, she exhaled. "That wasn't what I expected."

"Milady, one of these days, you'll trust me."

"I kind of liked it."

"Of course you did. I want to arouse you."

"Do it again?"

He did. He tapped her cunt until her whole body loosened.

"How do you like it?"

"More than I imagined I might."

He brushed her nipples with the flapper until they each hardened. As he continued, he used more pressure.

"I like," she said.

"Sorry?"

She realized she'd mumbled. "I like it."

"Ready for more?"

"I don't know. Am I?"

"Tell me if you're not."

But she was. The hits came faster and he mixed it up, striking her breasts, her belly, her pussy, her inner thighs.

She understood how it could be used differently to cause anguish, even damage, but in the hand of a master, this was ultimate seduction.

"Let go," he told her.

"I did."

"Not yet you haven't."

His crop seemed to be everywhere at once, licking, biting, caressing.

She closed her eyes and allowed her head to loll forward.

She was aware of him saying something, but she had no idea what. Her body burned with the fire he created.

Her pussy felt hot and in response, she became damper. The juxtaposition surprised her.

"Yes, Milady. Orgasm from my beating."

She knew that wasn't possible, but she didn't have the energy to argue.

He cropped her swollen breasts and nipples.

Her body jerked and she screamed. But he was relentless, dragging sensation from deeper than it had ever been before. "Damien? Damien!"

"Take it." He tapped her cunt dozens of times, never ceasing.

"I…" She couldn't get there.

"What do you want?"

An orgasm. Him.

She arched forward when he blazed a path up her inner thighs, the squared-off end of the flapper nipping at her swollen clit. "Damn it."

"Tell me," he encouraged.

"I want to come."

"Ask."

His voice seemed to come from a long way off.

The whole time, he continued to work her body. There wasn't an inch of her skin that didn't zing with fever.

He went back to the gentle tapping on her pussy. After the recent blazes, this was maddeningly soft.

When she didn't respond, he used the leather to brutally lick her labia. She screamed. The louder her cries, the harder he hit. She yelled, tugged at her bonds, twisted her body. "I want to come! Fuck it, Sir, I want to come!"

She heard the crop clatter to the floor.

"That's it."

Then his fingers were in her pussy, and he pressed against her G-spot. He forced the orgasm from her, and she sobbed, desperate, frantic, grateful.

"Now, Milady, the fucking."

Damien undressed and put on a condom. "On your tiptoes."

She wouldn't have known it was possible, but he managed to drive his cock up inside her, fucking her while she was fully tied.

If she'd had any doubt before now, it was erased. Damien had dominated her. Thoroughly. Completely.

She realized that, in the throes, she'd used the word Sir as he'd requested at least a month ago. In the moment, it had been inevitable.

One of his arms around her back, the other on her butt, he bent his knees and surged up inside her, filling her desperate pussy.

"I... Yes."

"That's it, Catrina, that's it. Give me everything you have. Your respect, your trust, your submission."

He fucked her so hard, so deep, she had no choice. "Yes. Sir! Sir, sir, *sir*." She struggled in her bonds, wanting to touch him.

Seeming to know it, he kissed her, brought her more firmly against him.

That drove her madder. Her body was still sensitized from his crop, and the skin-to-skin abrasion made her wild.

He continued his generous assault, giving her more and more, shoving her over the edge.

She curled her toes as she dropped her head onto his shoulder. "Take me, Damien."

He tightened his grip as his movements became shorter. He gave a final thrust, then with a masculine, guttural sound, he pulsed inside her

She didn't mind the bruises she was sure to have on her ass. The desperation in his grip made it worthwhile.

He held her for a long time, her head on his shoulder, his arms looped around her.

"Thank you, Milady."

The way he held her combined with the way they breathed together created a pulsing intimacy.

His penis slowly softened and slid out of her. He drew back and placed a thumb beneath her chin. "Let me untie you."

He took his time, caressing her skin as he released each limb. He looked at her, skimming a mark he'd left on her breast. "I'll put some cream on that."

"It'll be fine," she said.

"I said I'll put some cream on it."

She nodded.

He grabbed a tube from the counter and came back. His ministration was heart-meltingly tender.

"How are you doing?" he asked.

"No worse for wear." Catrina smiled. "Thank you." Now that the moment had passed, she couldn't believe how exposed she'd allow herself to be.

They each dressed, and he didn't say much. Her stomach knotted. Tonight she'd been more open and vulnerable than she'd ever been with anyone, and it disturbed her. She'd released every inhibition, allowed herself to be mastered. And she didn't know what to think. Her brain felt as if it were filled with a red fog.

"After you, Milady."

With old-world manners, he held open the door and nodded, silently communicating that she should walk in front of him.

He showered with her, and the damnable man took such wonderful care of her that she wanted to stay here forever.

Before he'd even rinsed her off, he had her aroused. She rubbed her pussy against his thigh.

"I'll take care of you when we go to bed," he promised, turning off the faucet.

"You know, I've decided I hate this orgasm denial thing you do."

He exited the shower, grabbed two towels and wrapped the first around her shoulders. "Yeah?"

"Really hate it."

"I'm amenable to listening to your objections. I'm not likely to be swayed."

She towel dried her hair while he dressed in a pair of lightweight workout pants and worn-to-soft T-shirt.

"Wine?" he offered.

"Sparkling water. With lime, if we have it."

"We do. I'll have it ready for you in the living room."

After brushing her hair, she put on yoga pants and a sweater. Barefoot, she joined him on the couch. She rested her back against the arm, facing him, sitting cross-legged.

She accepted the water.

"You've been on edge all day. Yes, I've requested you delay your orgasm twice, but your reaction seems a little out of proportion. Is that what's really going on? Or is this a camouflage?"

Would she ever notice that in one of her subs? And if she did, would she probe deep enough to uncover the answer? Most likely not, she acknowledged. Her boys showed up and scened with her. She knew what they wanted and she did her best to provide it. In the future, she'd be considerably more aware.

She stared at the bubbles in her drink while he waited. "You're right," she acknowledged, shaking back her hair to look at him. "Yes, you've frustrated me sexually, and I know why you do it. You're keeping me keenly aware that I'm here as a sub. Is there a more decadent way to do that than control my pleasure?"

The emotions that had been swimming through her now threatened to swamp her.

Until now, she hadn't truly realized what she'd said to Gregorio. She was starting to care about Damien. But she wanted an equal relationship, not with someone who had that much power over her. She loved the scenes, the sex, the orgasms and especially the time they shared together, working in the same office, brainstorming, talking, an occasional smoldering kiss or quickie. Then the evenings, in front of the fire, followed by the way he took her to bed.

Now that she'd experienced it, she knew she'd miss it.

The longer she stayed, the harder it would be to leave.

"So submitting to me is still problematic to you?"

She nodded. "More and more."

He propped an ankle on his opposite knee and drummed his fingers on his thighs. By staying where he was, he gave her room to breathe. Again, he seemed to know what she needed without her saying a word.

"Why is that?"

"I'm a Domme. I understand your lessons, Damien, and I appreciate them. I understand the dynamic in a way I never did. And I have more responsibility to my subs and to the scene I create than I realized two weeks ago." And she'd learnt the importance of talking to her boys beforehand to build their anticipation for the scene, let it fill their minds to the point of obsession, making the culmination all the more powerful. "I will be a hell of a lot more judicious in my use of a crop and a cane, even when the sub asks me to use it."

Damien nodded.

"And probably more forceful with a belt. As Gregorio said that one day, I'd better not hit like a girl." She smiled, but he didn't.

He allowed the silence to build until tension layered the atmosphere. Finally, she was unable to tolerate it and she went on, "I appreciate everything you've done." She inhaled. Then, before she could change her mind and give him an even bigger part of her heart, she added, "I need to leave." Tears welled in her eyes.

"What are you scared of?" he asked quietly.

"Nothing." *Everything.* That she was in so deep that she'd never find her way back. And how stupid was that? He'd been up front in saying he didn't believe in love. Not that it mattered. He wouldn't choose a woman who couldn't—wouldn't—submit to him. "The two weeks will be up on Saturday, and this way I can get back, get settled in, be ready for work on Monday morning, and we can avoid hiding out up here while the Den has a houseful of guests."

"We could always attend."

"With me as your sub," she said, voice flat.

"Naturally. That was the nature of our agreement, Milady."

She shook her head. "Not happening."

"Your decision is made?"

"It is."

"Is this open for discussion?" he asked.

Catrina leaned forward to slide her glass of water onto the table. "No." Because if it was, she'd relent. Her clothes would be off, and his hands would be all over her. And she'd be begging for his lash. And that was perhaps the worst of all possible scenarios, creating more confusion. If she were a Domme, why did she crave him? "I need you to respect my decision. Please?"

He inhaled sharply. "Of course." He nodded. "You can have it as you wish, Milady."

She stood, and her knees threatened to buckle.

Resolved, she walked to her closet and started throwing her clothing into a bag.

He offered no help.

She didn't see him in the living room and disappointment shrouded her.

What had she expected? That he'd stride into the bedroom and tie her to the headboard as he had threatened more than once? But he was the consummate Dom. If she asked him to honor her desires, he would. She told herself that that was what she wanted.

He wasn't in his office, and she checked the security monitors. She didn't see him on any of them.

On automatic pilot, she disconnected her computer from the printer and started to clear out her desk.

She heard the firm sound of his footfall on the stairs and the file she'd been holding slipped from her nerveless fingers.

"I started your car," he told her. "For safety reasons, it would be smarter for you to stay here overnight. Or I could have Jeff drive you into Winter Park so you can stay at a hotel."

Always looking out for her. "Thanks. I'm good."

"You're determined, then?"

Not trusting that her voice wouldn't tremble, betraying her feelings, she nodded.

"In that case, I'll get your box." He slung her computer backpack over one shoulder then headed down the stairs, leaving her to grab her bag.

The car was in the driveway, the nose pointed toward the street, which meant he'd backed it out then turned it around so she could drive straight out. It was running and the wipers made lazy swipes across the windshield.

He opened her car door and she slid into the warmed cab. While he stowed her belongings in the trunk, she rolled down the window.

"Call if you need anything," he said, hands propped on the top of the car. "Anything. Remember that I'm always available to talk about things, discuss your fears."

"Thank you. There are some things you'd never be willing to compromise on."

"Send me a text when you get home."

"No."

"That wasn't a request. It's just common fucking courtesy, Milady," he said, his voice tight. "It's late. It's dark. It's against my better judgment to let you go. At least have the decency to let me know you're safe. It's either that or I follow you. Your choice."

"You're serious."

"What do you think?"

"I'll send you a message," she promised. She wondered if she'd ever won a battle with him.

As the lights of the Den faded in her rearview mirror, she shivered. She felt alone and lonely in ways she'd never experienced before this moment.

Chapter Ten

"You look like you could use a drink."

Damien glanced at Gregorio as he entered his office uninvited. "Any excuse?"

"I'm simply doing you a favor. It's what friends are for," Gregorio said, zeroing in on the sideboard with its secret panel.

"Friends are for drinking your most expensive alcohol?"

"Who else is going to suffer like that for you, Boss?"

Damien reached forwards and clicked a couple of keys on his computer. Obviously Catrina wasn't turning her car around and coming back, so staring at the feed from the outdoor cameras any longer was pointless. He replaced the dozens of pictures with a tranquil beach scene. Palm trees and hammocks were on the left hand side, with crystal blue waters and white sand on the other. It looked sun-drenched, and as far away from here as he was from Catrina.

"Maybe I should have made us something with rum instead," Gregorio suggested when he looked at the screens.

"This will work." Damien accepted the snifter then leaned back and propped his feet on his desk. Lost in thought, he warmed the glass in his palms.

"I take it Milady left us."

"The two weeks were almost up."

"I'm not surprised."

Obviously Gregorio, too, had seen the way her car fishtailed as she accelerated away from the property.

"Something to say, Gregorio?"

"Not at all, Boss." He lazed back, legs stretched in front of him, crossed at the ankles.

"Why are you not surprised?"

"I think you scared the hell out of her. It's one thing to scene with a Dom, even to be a trainee. It's another to given him your total submission."

"Spoken like the voice of experience."

"Yeah. It's demanding," Gregorio said. "Think about what you wanted from her. Were you satisfied with teaching her how to be a better Domme?"

Damien glanced up and stared at the beach screenshot without actually seeing it. That was a question he didn't want to answer.

When he'd goaded her into accepting his challenge, he'd wanted to crack her toughness to see the woman beneath. He'd wanted to master her. But at what cost to her?

He'd caught glimpses of her vulnerability, and he'd relentlessly pushed, forcing her to expose them while offering little to nothing back in return. He hadn't mentioned what he was feeling or experiencing, even when she'd talked with Gregorio. He'd had a second chance when she'd come back after her walk.

And then...

Christ.

She'd called him Sir when she'd submitted to his crop earlier. Catrina had transcended a barrier she'd been keeping between them, given him a gift, and instead of immediately acknowledging it, sweeping her into his arms after rewarding her with a powerful orgasm, he'd... Stayed in the scene. Kept his professional distance. Then, when he'd brought her upstairs, he'd assumed she was angry about the lack of an orgasm.

Even when she'd announced her intention of leaving, he'd invited her to attend Friday night's festivities at the Den.

In retrospect, he saw that she'd given him one last chance to redeem himself when she'd asked if it would be as his sub. Even if he couldn't have agreed to anything else, he could have discussed it with her rather than shutting down the conversation.

For someone reputed to be an excellent Dom, he'd screwed up. Bad. Who the hell had he been to think he could teach her anything?

"You're not the biggest fuckwad on the planet, Boss. Just seems that way."

"Was that supposed to help?"

Gregorio shrugged.

Damien cared about her more than he would have believed possible. And he'd figured they had plenty of time to discuss things, see if they could reach mutual accord.

Gregorio took a sip of the brandy. "Damn, this is good stuff. Not sorry to be drinking it, even at your expense."

"What are friends for?" Damien said dryly, repeating Gregorio's earlier words. With that, he motioned for Gregorio to refill his glass.

* * * *

"Oh, my Cat, it's one thing to lie to us," Evelyn said softly, "but you need to ask if you're lying to yourself."

Caught.

Catrina looked at her mother over a beer. They were having lunch at the same brew pub where she'd met them three weeks ago. Three weeks that could have been a lifetime. "How do you do that?"

Evelyn nodded. "Mothers know these things."

"Your eyes give you away," Milton added.

Just like Damien had said.

"Miltey!" Evelyn smacked his arm. "Don't tell her my secrets."

Catrina reached for a roll and tore a chunk off it. "Next you'll be admitting you really don't have eyes in the back of your head."

"Actually, those she does have," Milton said.

Catrina smiled for the first time since leaving the Den and its enigmatic owner. She hadn't been out of the house in over a week, and seeing her mother today, even if her appendage was with her, was something she'd needed.

"So not hearing from your gentleman friend does bother you?" Evelyn asked.

That was an understatement. It was as if a metal band had been wrapped around her chest, constricting her breathing. "Yes." She sighed. It relieved her not to pretend otherwise.

"You two were closer than you let on."

"I was." She dipped the piece of bread in some butter, but she didn't eat it. "Obviously he wasn't."

"He seemed smitten to me," Evelyn said. "He hasn't called at all?"

"He left me alone for a few days, but he's called twice."

"And what else?"

"A few text messages." Several, every day.

"And?" her mother prompted.

"That's it. End of story."

"So what are you going to do about it?"

"Move on with my life." But she was beginning to wonder if that were possible. She was miserable. He haunted her days and stalked her nights. She thought about him when she had to pour her own coffee in the morning. And when she masturbated, she fantasized about the way he'd wielded the crop on her body. He even intruded on her bath time when she remembered the way he'd slicked his hands with soap and run them over her body.

"You're not going to respond?"

"No." She'd considered it, but had ultimately decided not to. She needed to heal, and contacting him would be counterproductive. There was nothing left to be said. She wouldn't give up who she was ever again, and he could only be with a woman who subbed for him…if he were willing to fall in love again.

It was easier to tell herself that they had shared a fun couple of weeks.

She just wished she could convince herself not to miss his touch, and most of all, the magical intimacy.

Noticing that both her mother and Milton were looking at her expectantly, she blinked. "Did I miss something? Sorry."

Evelyn patted Catrina's hand. "I want you to be happy. You're one of the strongest people I know." She softened her voice. "It's okay to take your own advice. Protect yourself." She shrugged. "But you're allowed to fall in love again."

She wished it were that simple.

"You risk being hurt. I don't blame you for wanting to avoid that. But there's a lot of joy to be had out there, too." She looked at her future husband. "And there are no guarantees." Evelyn's tone soothed, taking any sting out of her words.

"Unless he's done something dastardly?" Milton asked.

"No. Nothing like that."

"He's not a liar or a cheat?"

She shook her head.

"Then ask yourself if you're trying to avoid failure."

Catrina sat there, shocked into silence. Was that true?

"That's not you at all, my Cat. Not at all. At least talk to your young man." She gave a final pat. "The way he tied his hair back…that was hot."

"Mother!

"Evelyn!"

Evelyn giggled and sipped her beer. "I'm about to be married, not buried, my darling Miltey. I notice these things." Then she batted her eyes at him. "Not that there will ever be any other man on the planet for me."

Until today, the last time her mother had embarrassed her, Catrina had been in middle school. She shook her head to clear the image. "Wedding. Details. Did you decide on"—she so did not want to hear about the honeymoon—"what flowers you'll decorate the chapel with?"

Milton signaled to the server that he'd like another beer and patiently sat back to listen while her mother bubbled over with excitement. His obvious fondness and tolerance of Evelyn's enthusiasm endeared him to Catrina. Maybe Damien had been right about that, too.

After dinner, she drove home, and her phone dinged, signaling another incoming text message. With Damien's tone.

She ignored it, too.

This evening, one of her subs was coming over and she needed to get the house, and herself, prepared. Ridiculously, as she did so, she couldn't help but think about Damien.

Keeping his coaching in mind, she'd sent her boy several e-mails, building the tension. They'd had a couple of phone conversations, and she'd explored what he liked in greater depth than they ever had before. Shaun had told her how grateful he was.

And she had no doubt he meant it. Damien's constant sex talk when they'd been together had kept her on edge.

Shaun arrived right on time and, instead of taking him directly to her play room as she always had in the past, she instructed him sit on a chair in her living room. She walked around him, softly talking, bouncing her paddle off her thigh as she went.

She'd been shocked how unnatural it had seemed to dress up in her Domme make-up. She'd grown accustomed to Damien selecting her attire, and she'd agonized over choosing the right outfit. Instead of a skirt that would leave her ass exposed, she'd covered up with shiny black shorts. She'd left her legs bare, but her boots went up past her knees.

Feeling like dressing more modestly than she sometimes did, she'd fought her way into a black corset accented with white leather insets that made her waist look impossibly small.

Shaun's gaze was transfixed on her. He sat with his back straight, twisting his hands in his lap. He wore black leather chaps, and his cock was already hard and weeping. Generally by this point in a scene, she would already be getting aroused, but not tonight. All she could think about was Damien and the way her pulse roared when he circled her. Part of her wished that she, rather than Shaun, were sitting in that chair. "The bench for you, I think, hmm?" she asked. "I can bend you over it and tie those wrists to the opposite side. That will get your ass up in the air for me." She stopped in front of him. She took the handle of the paddle and put it beneath his chin to tip back his head. Leaning toward him, she softly asked, "Won't it, Shaun?"

He gulped. "Yes, Milady."

"How red is it going to be, boy?"

When he didn't immediately answer, she dropped the paddle and smacked the side of his leg. She knew the leather would deaden the impact, but the sound was startling.

He jumped.

"How red, boy?" she snapped.

"Very, Milady. As much as you want. Oh, please."

Pounding on the front door shattered her carefully constructed scene.

"What the hell?" Shaun asked, leaping up.

She blinked. She wasn't expecting anyone. "I'm sure they have the wrong house. Now where were we?"

His cock had softened a little, and she silently cursed the unseen person. *Damn it.* She'd all but had him mesmerized...

The pounding continued. "Sorry," she said. "I'll sort it—"

"Open up the fucking door, Milady!"

She froze. *Damien?*

"Now."

He'd shredded her nerves. "I'll be right with you, love," she promised Shaun. "Wait there." She put the paddle on the table then ran a finger down his cheekbone in a motion she hoped was reassuring.

But Shaun jumped up and reached for his coat.

Trying for a calm she was nowhere close to feeling, she strode to the door, paddle still in hand. Despite the fact her outfit would shock the neighbors, she jerked the door open. "How dare you, you jackass—"

All her angry protests died. All she saw was a wall of red roses.

He moved them aside. "We need to talk. I texted you that I was coming. Invite me in."

"I'm busy here."

"Invite me in," he repeated, "or I'll drag your ass out here in the cold in front of anyone who passes by and we can have our discussion out there…"

He looked around. A couple were coming down the street with their dog.

"Your timing sucks. Come back in an hour." She tried to slam the door—that would be satisfying—but he angled his foot on the threshold. "Damn you."

With inexorable determination he moved forwards, forcing her to back up.

Then he shut the door.

"Master Damien?"

His gaze settled on Shaun. "Did I interrupt something?"

"I tried to tell you that," she said, hands on her hips.

He put the flowers on the couch. They covered two cushions. "There's a VIP event at the Den tomorrow night. Not open to the public," he said to Shaun. "I'll put you on the list. And I'll sign you up for a session with Gregorio. On me."

"Rad."

"Now, out."

"Yes, Sir," Shaun said.

She seethed while Damien ushered the man out. "Who the hell do you think you are, barging into my home, throwing out my guests, interrupting my life?" She strode toward him. "I told you weeks ago I was happy to put the smack down on your arrogant ass. And I'm ready to do it right now, this fucking minute."

"Really?" he asked, voice smooth, silky soft. Lethal with its restrained power. "Is that what you want, Milady? Really?"

As he advanced, she stood her ground though instinct warned her to retreat.

He caught her hair and wrapped it around his hand. She remembered her safe word, but couldn't force herself to use it.

"Or do you want to hear me say I love you?"

The floor spun beneath her. "What?"

"Or do you want to hear that I was an idiot that night in my dungeon?"

"Which night? There was more than one," she said.

To his credit, he ignored that comment. "You know what I'm talking about. When you called me Sir."

"It was a scene," she insisted.

He nodded. "It meant nothing?"

"It meant I respected you," she hedged.

"It meant you submitted to me," he challenged.

"No. I…"

"Stop. Now. Give me the honest truth, Catrina."

"That was the truth."

"You looked down and to the left. I'm calling bullshit on your answer."

Adrenaline knocked the wind out of her.

"Look me in the eyes," he said tightly. "And have a grown-up conversation with me. You don't like where it goes, then I'll leave and you won't hear from me again. Fair?"

"Have a seat," she said.

"I'd rather stand."

"And I'd rather you sat." She stood there, resolved. She needed the distance between them, needed him not to tower over her where she was aware of his power, the musky scent of him that spoke to something entirely too female in her.

It took two swipes for him to move all the roses aside.

Hardly able to string two coherent thoughts together, she said, "I'll be right back with you." She went into her bedroom for the thickest, fluffiest, most unflattering robe she owned. She knotted the belt around her waist then gave it an extra tug for good measure.

With a deep breath, Catrina took a moment to compose herself. *Love?* Did he mean it? And so what if he did? She wasn't changing who she was for any man.

It might have been easier to convince herself of her resolve if she hadn't stopped breathing when he'd said those words.

She closed her eyes, arming herself with determination, then went back to the living room. He'd taken off his coat and he sat there as if he had every right to occupy her space.

And damn it, his hair was tied back, all sexy like her mom had said.

Pretending to be unaffected, she sat in a chair across from him. "I can spare five minutes."

"You're lucky I don't pull down your pants and spank your ass until you get real with me."

He stood but resumed his seat when she nodded toward the couch. Instead, he leaned forward, elbows on his thighs and cradling his head. "Look, Milady, I screwed up. I let you leave when I shouldn't have."

"Don't be a martyr. You tried to stop me."

"Before that. Before you had the need to run. I had chances to talk to you, but I ignored them. I told you I didn't believe in love. I didn't."

She inclined her head. "And now?"

"I haven't been able to get you out of my mind. When I realized how empty the Den was without you, I went back home. And that's when I figured it out."

Holding back a dozen questions, she waited.

"My life is empty without you. I want to share my days and nights with you. I want you to share your dreams and fears with me."

Heart thundering, breaking, she bravely said, "It would never work. D/s would be a problem for us."

"How so?"

"Did you pay any attention to me over the two weeks we spent together?"

"Every word, nuance, plea, moan, whimper. Along with a few screams."

"Then you'd know that I can't be a sub."

"Won't," he contradicted.

"Can't," she insisted.

"My touch does nothing for you?"

"You know it does."

"The way I build a scene doesn't leave you breathless with anticipation?"

"Of course it does."

"Then where's the problem?"

"I can't fit into a typical D/s relationship."

"There's no such thing." He came to his feet.

She supposed she should have been grateful he'd harnessed his energy as long as he had.

"I think you have an idea that D/s has to mean something specific."

"It doesn't to you?"

"Just as every relationship is different, so is the way the couple treats D/s. I like beating your ass. I like bringing you off slow. I like the way you writhe and scream. I like the way you called me Sir."

"That was a slip."

"I agree. But it was an honest one. Your defenses were down. It was one of the most real moments we've shared."

A chill held her spine rigid.

"Don't diminish it by denying it."

It scared her how easily he could read her. It had meant something. And even she didn't want to believe that. "Okay." She tried for flippant. "But I also love chocolate. And I refuse to eat it more than once a month because it makes my butt bigger. And the more I get, the more I want."

"More truth, Milady. You want it. You want me. You want my domination."

She shook her head and knotted the tie more carefully.

"You just don't want to get hurt again. You want someone you can lean on, trust, who will be there for you. And you think that if you get on your knees for me and call me Sir, all of the other disappears. But it doesn't have to. What if you can have it all, Catrina? Love and submission. Respect and security?"

"I'm not sure what you're saying."

"We're good together. Even if you submit in our sex life, it doesn't mean I require it of you in public. I will always treat you like a lady and invite you into the inner circle of my life, my plans, goals and ideas."

She didn't know what to say.

It astounded her that he'd sorted it all out, even when she hadn't. Yes, the word Sir had been a slip, but he'd caught the significance. Not as quickly, maybe, as she would have liked. And instead of letting it feed his ego or shoving it aside, he'd pursued her. He'd tried to give her the space to come to him, but in the end, he'd relentlessly tracked her down.

He'd taken the time to figure out what he wanted and was willing to give. And he'd thought about her and how to give her what she needed.

"I've heard you coach your clients. I'm willing for us to exchange financial plans...whatever you need to feel comfortable. All I need in return is the word Sir spoken of your own free will."

"I've got to have room to think." Which wasn't easy with him standing there and with the overwhelming scent of flowers permeating the air.

"I understand. I'll give you five seconds."

"You are impossible."

"I am who I am."

She knew the next words without him saying them. "You know what you want."

Tension radiated through his shoulders. A pulse throbbed in his temples. She'd thought he was determined, two-hundred pounds of unstoppable Dom. But now she glimpsed beneath his gruff exterior and saw the raw truth exposed in the stark blue depths of his eyes.

The Big Bad Dom was nervous. This — she — they — mattered that much to him?

The truth was, she'd become a Domme to close herself off, to protect her emotions from hurt, much as he'd guessed a month ago.

Tonight, with Shaun, the kick she used to get out of dominating a man was missing.

She wanted to be the focus of someone's attention. And not just someone's. Damien's.

"I love you, Milady Catrina," he said again, voice hoarse with emotion.

At one time, she'd wanted to shake him up. She'd gotten what she wanted. His honesty was emotionally raw. In this moment, he seemed as shattered as she was. "I don't know how this works," she admitted.

"Me either. D/s is a power exchange. I only have the power you give me. You have ultimate control."

She frowned.

"I'm humbled. I am here because I need you, want you. I desire you for your intellect and your strength. I was mad with jealousy when I thought of you and Gregorio sceneing together."

"I told you it was a joke."

"I had never felt anything like that before. You matter. You, Catrina. I know we can work it out together. And I know I'm better with you by my side. We've had a decent track record of talking to each other. Come to me with your fears and doubts."

"You're asking a lot."

He took one step toward her, the first step.

Then he waited. His intent was clear. Whatever happened next was up to her. Her heart raced, and a hundred emotions collided inside her soul.

Closing the distance scared her. But the idea of a future without him was bleak and dark. Did she dare risk what he was offering?

She took a large, symbolic one toward him.

And he was there, meeting her, capturing her, holding her, kissing her.

"I will protect, honor, cherish you, Catrina."

"And give me dozens of orgasms?"

"That seems like a good place to begin."

"Begin, Sir?"

"Tell me you love me, Milady. It might not be easy, but together we can sort the rest out."

"I…" She shook. "I do love you, Damien."

"Every day, I will earn it."

She lifted onto her tiptoes even as he unknotted her belt.

"You're mine," he said, impatiently removing her robe and loosening her corset.

"Yours," she agreed, mastered.

About the Author

Sierra Cartwright was born in Manchester, England and raised in Colorado. Moving to the United States was nothing like her young imagination had concocted. She expected to see cowboys everywhere, and a covered wagon or two would have been really nice!

Now she writes novels as untamed as the Rockies, while spending a fair amount of time in Texas…where, it turns out, the Texas Rangers law officers don't ride horses to roundup the bad guys, or have six-shooters strapped to their sexy thighs as she expected. And she's yet to see a poster that says Wanted: Dead or Alive. (Can you tell she has a vivid imagination?)

Sierra wrote her first book at age nine, a fanfic episode of Star Trek when she was fifteen, and she completed her first romance novel at nineteen. She actually kissed William Shatner (Captain Kirk) on the cheek once, and she says that's her biggest claim to fame. Her adventure through the turmoil of trust has taught her that love is the greatest gift. Like her image of the Old West, her writing is untamed, and nothing is off-limits.

She invites you to take a walk on the wild side…but only if you dare.

Sierra Cartwright loves to hear from readers. You can find her contact information, website details and author profile page at http://www.totallybound.com.

Totally Bound Publishing

Made in the USA
Lexington, KY
05 September 2014